The Shepherd Boy

The Shepherd Boy

A NOVEL BY

Darick Allan

PORTAL PRESS
WASHINGTON, D.C.

The following is a work of fiction. Any resemblance to actual events, or persons, living or dead, is entirely coincidental.

Published in the United States of America

Library of Congress Control Number: 2005904828
ISBN 10: 1-933454-01-6
ISBN 13: 978-1-933454-01-6

Portal Press
1327 Irving Street, N.E.
Washington, D.C. 20017
www.theportalpress.com

To MLE

The Shepherd Boy

Chapter One

THE TWO BOYS CAME TO A TURN IN THE ROAD and rested awhile before continuing uphill. They were on a mission. Already they were among the houses that were being built above their own neighborhood, and though this was where they normally played, they were planning a greater adventure than usual. Their destination was the plateau on top of the mountain where an Indian boy was watching some sheep. It was a Wednesday afternoon the second week of school, and they hadn't let go of summer.

"I'm going to get that bastard," said the taller boy, who was rather harmless looking. He was nine years old.

His name was Tommy Montovan. He was an American, and his best friend Geoffrey O'Donnell was Irish. Being Irish wasn't nearly as impressive as being American (both boys agreed on this point), but it was better than being poor; and they lived in the finest neighborhood in Quito. They were both from diplomatic families, and like most children in the aristocracy of a poor country, they had a feeling that they were different from other people and had a special role to play in the world.

"That bloody son of a bitch!" exclaimed Geoffrey indignantly. It was exciting to use language that was so dangerous around his mother.

The pavement came to an end a few yards ahead. A dirt road, carved out of the side of the mountain like a small canyon, continued uphill and wound back and forth through the scattered construction sites: some of the houses were nearly completed; the shells of others were seemingly abandoned. Each of the sites had a guard whose job was to make sure none of the pipes or bricks piled next to the shells were carted off by thieves. Tommy waved at a watchman named Manuel, who was wearing a dark blue uniform and stood in front of a fascinating, three-storey hulk; but Manuel apparently did not feel a need to wave back, and, alerted to the boys' presence, watched them with a singular alertness devoid of curiosity.

"How can he treat animals like that?" asked Tommy, referring to the shepherd boy who was not yet in sight.

"We're going to get him—we bloody will!" replied Geoffrey. "Let me have some water."

They drank from a canteen hanging from Tommy's belt. It was a ritual that fortified the idea that they were about to do something important, and they tasted the water solemnly. Then they continued uphill under the watchful eyes of Manuel, who realized they would not be disturbing him that day.

Their hearts were united in a murderous rage. Its exhilaration wasn't much different from their excitement during the war games Tommy led at the construction sites after school, but this was the first time they actually meant to hurt someone. In Tommy's mind attacking the shepherd boy was the right thing to do; and behind his thinking was a romantic notion of the Lord and His creatures. His ideas about Christianity were taken little from the Bible itself. Instead he drew from Sunday school stories about shepherds visited by angels, and pictures of Christ in the manger surrounded by gentle animals welcoming His promise into the world. Since the death of his mother two years before Tommy relied on that promise: for Jesus was his constant, invisible companion, salving his loneliness, listening even now as he thought, "We're almost there; I'm going to do what's right; I'm going to be brave!"

Chapter One

The road meandered a hundred paces above the most recent construction site, making its last claim upon nature. Beyond it was a slope of rough grass turning yellow and brittle in the final month of the dry season. The boys climbed strenuously, stopping one last time to share the canteen.

The austere beauty of the mountaintop at nine thousand feet was like a Bible setting come alive. The plateau was a grazing area for cattle and sheep, and there were few trees at that altitude to cut off the presence of the blue sky. The poor cholos who led the cattle up to pasture in the mornings weren't far removed from the Hebrew shepherds of Tommy's favorite stories, and as he watched them pass his house, they became living illustrations of seekers walking up to commune with God. He believed in the premise implicit in every Bible tale: that each life is blessed, and that a thrilling and unique destiny awaits us all.

Like many children who live in their imagination, however, Tommy had more sympathy for animals than people, and he was shocked by the casual cruelty of the Indians to their livestock. From his garden he saw it every day: the cholos whacked the animals with staves, yelled at them and kicked; and Tommy's thoughts followed the creatures as they lumbered up to the wild grass above his neighborhood. In his mind the cholos were arrogant and needed to learn the gentleness of the creatures they had tamed. That was why, one late afternoon, he set aside Christian teachings of tolerance and filled his pockets with stones. The two boys reached the eastern edge of the plateau brimming with conviction, and saw the great villain of their plot sitting about a hundred yards away.

The villain was a dirty boy of eleven who had not been fed well enough to reach the stature of his new enemies. He was sitting on a large boulder in the middle of a field dotted with other large rocks and about twenty suffering sheep. The sheep were used to suffering. The right rear leg of each was bent cruelly at the knee, and then tied, so that ankle and thigh were squeezed together. Another rope led from the bound leg to a stake in the ground. This made them three-legged creatures easy to control and that is why they were left in the care of a small boy. The villain thought of the sheep in a purely utilitarian way, and was oblivious to the pain in their back legs, or how cruel it was to force them into purposeful lives that ended in the slaughter-house. His clothes were too large for him and might have fit a boy several years older. He was wearing a floppy hat, a tattered red poncho, and dilapidated rubber boots that he was swinging casually, out of boredom, when he saw the two golden-haired boys gain the edge of the plateau.

The golden-haired boys looked like little gods to him. They wore fresh, brightly colored clothes and had the unmistakable confidence of children blessed with fortune. He wondered why they were staring at him. The villain understood how rarely rich foreign boys associated with Indians, but felt anticipation when he saw they were taking real notice of him, and stopped moving his legs. Finally the taller of the blondes crossed his arms and yelled to him.

"You bastard!"

The Indian did not know what this meant. He noted the hostile tone of the boy, but figured that it was a greeting of some kind, and that he might answer it. He was naïve enough to believe that the rich children might want to become friendly with him, and buoyancy entered his heart. But his round face remained impassive, unwilling to betray his more optimistic nature.

"Son of a bitch!" shouted the second of the boys.

The villain did not understand this either, and was not oblivious to the possibility that he was being taunted. But he did not see any reason for the rich boys to have anything against him, and with a faint hope he waved at them as nonchalantly as he could.

The two gods stared back with expressions that were very hard to read. Finally the taller boy screamed in Spanish.

"Hijo de puta!"

The Indian understood the meaning of these words very clearly. He understood, literally, that he was being called a son of a whore, but he did not understand why. A chill came over him as he realized the other boys despised him. They did not hate him with any good reason, and he felt his heart contract. They looked down on him because he was a poor and dirty Indian and there was nothing he could do about it. His body stiffened with the shock of sudden humiliation. But his face remained as impassive as before.

"Cabrón!" screamed Geoffrey, as the gods quickly depleted their vocabulary of dirty Spanish.

The Indian boy began to cry. His tears were those of a child who had not received much sympathy and did not expect much. They trickled down his cheeks, taking some of the dirt off his face, which added to the bitter salty flavor that reached his lips. Because his crying was so restrained, it didn't purge his feelings so much as add to his humiliation.

The rich boys continued shouting at the villain without any visible effect. It didn't occur to Tommy or his friend that *"cabrón"* or *"hijo de puta"* didn't convey what their mission was about. The Indian was supposed to know that torturing sheep was wrong and that he was being punished accordingly. But from a hundred yards away he seemed to be staring back impudently.

Tommy felt uncomfortable. Though his plan called for freeing the sheep and beating up the Indian if possible, he was frightened by the kid's insolence and began to wonder if he was going to get into trouble. He was also afraid of his stepmother, and letting a bunch of sheep loose was the sort of action that led to consequences. Unfortunately, since Geoffrey had seen him put rocks in his pockets, it would seem cowardly if he didn't use them. So he decided to proceed with the mission a little longer, not because he wanted to hurt the Indian or had any intention of rescuing the sheep. He simply didn't want to be a coward.

"All right. We're going to have to get closer. You go over there to the left, and I'll go straight. When we get to those rocks we attack. Good luck!"

"That little bugger," replied Geoffrey, "Right!"

The boys ran toward their prey, crouched over slightly as they did when avoiding squirt gun shots in a war game. As he got closer to the Indian, Tommy felt a surge of adrenalin and drowned out his uneasiness with thoughts of how evil the Indian was. By the time he was twenty feet away he had convinced himself that what he was about to do was just. He stopped, put his right hand in his pocket, and threw its contents in the general direction of the boy watching the sheep.

The first stones were just pebbles and fell lightly around the Indian, who continued sitting rigidly. If he wanted to react or run away, he didn't have time to anyway, for as Geoffrey shouted, "Bugger! Bugger! Bugger!" from behind a large boulder, Tommy reached down instinctively for another weapon. Feeling through the grass, he selected a heavy rock with a sharp ridge and threw it at the shepherd. Suddenly the Indian boy was clutching the side of his face, screaming, "Ay! Ay! Ay!"

"You cut his cheek open, Tommy! You cut his cheek open! Look at that!"

"Let's go, let's go, let's go!"

The gods ran back to edge of the plateau, abandoning the Indian to his wound and completely forgetting about the sheep. A few of the creatures, however, bleated "M-maa-maa! M-maa-aaa!" They knew something was wrong and slowly formed a circle around their master as he curled up on the ground.

By the time the boys reached the construction sites they slowed down so as not to appear suspicious. Geoffrey was excited. He had not actually thrown any rocks, and so did not feel very guilty about the cholo boy. But he was an accomplice to the crime nonetheless, and his closeness to the situation was thrilling. He felt sympathy for Tommy, who had a lot to cover up, and who was his best friend after all. His sympathy for the Indian was more abstract, and he generally felt the boy got what he deserved.

Tommy felt awful. He hadn't meant to hurt the Indian boy, and found the gravity of his crime almost incomprehensible. He was praying all the way down the path, "Oh Jesus, please forgive me, please forgive me!" He felt so sorry for what he had done that he was willing to do almost anything to atone for it—except, of course, be found out. His mind was already full of projects to secretly bring food to the boy's family. He felt very lonely, and was reminded that his mother was dead and that only God could be a witness to his true feelings and nature. Beneath all of this, however, was an unfamiliar pride, not for what he had done, but for the fact that he had done something. It reinforced the idea that his destiny was unique.

They passed under the gaze of Manuel again, and this time the boys felt so compelled to act innocent that they waved at him with extraordinary eagerness. Manuel lifted one hand perfunctorily, and watched them descend toward the exclusive homes at the highest reach of the Avenida Bolivar.

Tommy's house was only a block below the construction sites, at the apex of the avenida, and when it came in sight, Tommy put his hand on Geoffrey's shoulder and said: "Geoffrey, *please*. Don't tell! Don't tell!"

"I won't tell anybody, Tommy."

"Nobody!"

"Not my mom. Not my sister."

"Nobody at school!"

"Not anybody," agreed Geoffrey solemnly.

The boys shared the canteen again in acknowledgment of their pact, and shortly afterwards said goodbye at the intersection of the new road with the avenida. Geoffrey continued walking downhill as Tommy stood facing his house from across the street. When the Irish boy was about a hundred feet away, he turned and waved at Tommy one last time. Later in life the boys moved to separate countries and more or less forgot about each other, but that moment stayed with them both as the one in which they were the best of friends and shared a secret with no one else on earth.

Chapter Two

Moments later Tommy arrived at the gates to his house and rang a doorbell under the name Aguillar. The Aguillars were a wealthy landowning family who had built the house several years earlier on such a commanding height that the blue awning outside the dining room window could be seen for miles from the city below. But they had only lived in the house briefly before migrating to one of their properties in the countryside. Since then they had rented the place at ruinous prices to a variety of foreigners. The name remained above the doorbell, however, and was a constant reminder to the American family inside, with their pets and servants, that their residence was temporary.

The bell sounded in the kitchen and Rafael, who was in the middle of chopping an onion, peered through a slit-shaped window. "Here comes the general with his canteen!" he remarked good-naturedly to Mariella. "What do you think he does in the hills all day with that little friend of his, eh?" He cocked an eye mischievously at his wife, but his gesture was met with a sour expression, and he did not pursue the point.

The cook pressed a button, a buzzer sounded outside, and Tommy pushed open the gate. He followed a walkway that passed through an extraordinary garden on its way to the front door. The arrangement and care of the plants was the work of a dedicated full-time gardener, although it was mostly appreciated by an abundance of spoiled cats. A variety of bright flowers lined the walkway as well as the perimeter of the wall; the lawn itself was dotted with guava trees. Tommy often played on the edge of the flowerbeds and knew the smell and texture of individual geraniums and daisies intimately, but he got no pleasure out of the garden now. His only relief was noticing that the Rambler in the carport was gone, and with it the formidable presence of his stepmother Miriam. He had a feeling that God was watching him, and carried that miserable self-consciousness with him toward the house.

A fat, shorthaired cat named Whitey, who had been hiding among the flowers, jumped out when he became aware of the boy and approached him with an erect tail. With what tenderness did Tommy greet the cat! He felt the approach of the animal as a balm of forgiveness, and thought that petting him might alleviate his guilt. He was very kind to animals, and unlike other children his age who treated pets with rough affection, he had a particular gentleness the cat found soothing.

"You're a very good cat, Whitey," he reassured the creature authoritatively. "A very good cat. I hope you haven't been eating bugs. Bugs are not good for you at all. You must have been lying in the dirt. Look how dirty your stomach is! *Good* cat, good cat."

Whitey signaled a change in mood with a twitch in his spine, and lay on his back. He presented his stomach to the boy, as well as a disposition that was suddenly playful and malicious. Tommy, who knew enough to realize that petting the cat's stomach would turn him into a biting and scratching beast, stood up with disappointment. He looked briefly around the garden. Normally he would have stopped to investigate the flowerbeds, looking for beetles and pretending to have adventures on exotic planets. But the moment the rock struck the Indian's cheek kept playing in his mind. He tried escaping into the house.

He entered rather noisily, wiped his shoes, and yelled out a greeting to the cook.

"There he is!" came the amused reply.

Tommy peered down the hallway into the kitchen, catching a glimpse of the back of Rafael, who was still working diligently on the onions. Mariella, sitting with a bowl of unopened pea pods on her lap, greeted him with a solemn stare.

Tommy decided to go to his room. He glanced into the den by the front door, purely out of habit, and went directly for the stairs. These he jumped down two at a time with an affected boisterousness that made him even more miserable. At the landing where the stairs turned he paused at a great window that looked out on the yard. Its sill was decorated with sea-objects. The sea horse and starfish fascinated him particularly, and he wondered, as he had many times before, what their life had been at the bottom of the sea. But even that soothing curiosity went nowhere.

If anything, he felt worse in his room. His brother Billy wasn't there to distract him, and the familiar presence of his toys merely reminded him that he was a different person than he had been only a couple of hours before. He heard his sister moving around her bedroom, and decided to visit her, hoping vaguely that she would comfort him.

One of the effects of his stepmother's tyrannical regime was that the children no longer trusted one other very much. Miriam had a particularly cruel method of calling each child to her room individually and asking detailed questions about the others—she was concerned about a bewildering array of crimes, and at least one child was punished every day. Though none of the kids had actually betrayed anyone, an atmosphere of suspicion had arisen between them, broken regularly by nostalgia for the days when their mother was alive.

His sister reminded him more than anyone of his mother, and not only for the obvious reasons that she was a girl and older than him. Katy had inherited most of their mother's effects. Her room was decorated in a comforting, feminine way with carved animal figures their mother had collected in Africa as well as mementos from her childhood in Sweden. Among them was a herd of old plastic horses that she treasured along with dreams of having her own pony. She had also inherited her mother's dry sense of humor, which she practiced on her youngest brother with frequent and gentle stabs. She was fifteen years old.

Tommy found her sitting on her bed cutting her toenails. She looked at him slyly. "Hello, Thomas-us. Are you back from your expedition? I heard you slam that door. You always slam doors around here after you've been shooting people." She seemed gladdened by his presence, but did not let it distract her from her fascinating toes.

Tommy was aware of the condescension in her voice, and the faint plan he had of confessing his crime to her was entirely frustrated. He slumped into a chair by the window. "Oh, I was just playing," he replied irritably.

Katy did not reply immediately, but looked at him obliquely as she studied another one of her toes. From the attention she paid to her feet and her fine ankles, it was obvious she was intoxicated with vanity. She had a crush on a boy who played soccer at school, and her fantasy life was full of fascinating variations on encounters with him. Her awareness of her beauty helped insulate her from the prison-like atmosphere at home, but it could not protect her entirely from the humiliations imposed by her stepmother. Miriam forced her to wear clothes appropriate for a girl three years younger, and she was not allowed to go out with her girlfriends.

"Are you thinking about Mommy, Thomas-us?" asked Katy sympathetically.

The boy, for want of anything else to say, replied that he was, and his sister got up and began handling the figurines. She described with a definite authority how their mother had acquired each one. It was a sentimental ritual with the girl, and was usually a satisfying exercise for the boy as well. But it only reminded him now that his mother had been watching him from

Heaven, and might not love him after what he had done.

Katy noticed his tense, abstracted expression and thought: "Poor boy. What on earth is wrong?" Tact kept her from probing any further, however, and a few minutes later Tommy left her room.

In his tortured mind an idea occurred to him. It would not make up for his injury to the shepherd, but might prove to God that he was capable of good works. He decided to enlighten the cook on a favorite subject of his; for much as he liked Rafael (and feared his wife), he considered both exceedingly ignorant.

He made his way to the hallway in the servants' quarters, where the cat litter boxes were kept, and bounded up the back staircase to the kitchen. He settled on a stool at a long counter across from the refrigerator and looked out the window at a vacant lot with a steep slope of grass and brush. Tommy was doing his best to look innocent, and with the open quality of his blue eyes set against his smooth, freckled face, it was an easy guise.

"Ah! There he is again! And what can I do for you, young sir?" asked the cook, who was wiping his hands on an apron. He was the only one of the servants to wear a uniform: though it wasn't required of him, he found it a useful way to separate his private life from his job.

"Can I have cinnamon toast?"

"Mm," replied the cook painfully. The upper half of his face fell rather dramatically into the lower half.

"Not allowed," piped in Mariella with her bitter voice. "The Señora said no sweets in the afternoon—of any kind—only fruits."

"True enough, my friend," continued Rafael apologetically. "It's not allowed. But if you want fruit—why there it is on top of the refrigerator. And if you want—" Here the cook shrugged his shoulders blithely, as if to imply that any request would be a cinch to fulfill—as long as the Señora allowed it.

"May I have some tea and a banana?" asked the boy.

Rafael lit up with an exaggerated display of happiness, and his wife returned gravely to her work with the pea pods. Within minutes the kettle was hot, and the cook came back with a fresh cup of tea.

Of course Tommy was not concerned with the tea or the banana; he was simply warming up his audience for their further education. Rafael leaned on the counter watching the boy, and his solid rectangular face, etched with sad Indian features, settled into an expression of unassuming dignity.

"Would you like to hear about the United States Apollo space program?" asked the boy casually. "I have some pictures downstairs."

"Would I like to hear about the United States Apollo?" repeated the cook expansively. "Well—certainly!" He turned to his wife with another of his incredulous, wide-eyed expressions, and received a contemptuous snort in reply. Rafael was beginning to believe he'd stumbled onto an ideal situation—one that would allow him to simultaneously humor the boy and bait his wife.

Tommy returned momentarily with a copy of National Geographic and an outdated book called *You Will Go to the Moon*. He opened the magazine officiously and pointed to the launch facility at Cape Kennedy as well as an illustration showing the flight path of the first mission. "We're sending a man to the moon in two years," the boy explained carefully. "The rocket is taking off there—in Florida—and then it takes three days to go to the moon. But first they have to orbit the moon, and then they land in the Landing Module—see?"

"They have to go *around* the moon first?" observed the cook, who thought the whole procedure rather arbitrary.

"Yes," replied the boy. "The moon is round, you know."

"No!"

"Yes. The earth is round too."

"Round! Did you hear that, Mariella? The earth is *round*,"

said the cook gleefully. His wife glared at them both. She was completely unable to admire her husband's sense of humor, and rarely smiled except in situations of extreme irony that confirmed her pessimistic view of God's Plan on Earth. She was hoping La Señora would come home so that her husband would stop behaving like a fool.

"Christopher Columbus discovered that the earth is round," continued the boy in a faltering manner. The sideshow of the cook grinning at his wife was beginning to distract from the lesson, and he began to wonder if the couple's ignorance was really as pitiable as it appeared. Tommy suspected the cook was making fun of him, but was mollified when Rafael looked at the magazine with humility, and said, "The United States can do just about anything, can't it? It's very rich, isn't it, my friend?"

Mariella's wish was granted soon enough. They heard the Rambler pause outside the carport, and at the clinking of the gates Tommy, without saying goodbye, rushed down the back stairs with the magazine and the book. His disappearance was no surprise to Rafael or the sullen woman operating on the peas.

Once downstairs Tommy wasn't sure what to do with himself. He returned the magazine and the book to his room, but couldn't bear the thought of remaining there. He felt too guilty, and knew he would act nervous if Miriam looked in. So he decided to go outside, and went through the servants' quarters to the back door. As he sneaked past the stairway, he could hear his stepmother setting down bags of groceries, laughing harshly with the servants. "Ha ha ha! Ha ha ha !" It was a forced, superior laugh, and it frightened the boy.

In the back yard he felt the balm of nature, and it comforted him. The back was on a lower terrace than the entrance to the house; a stone staircase built into a wall was the only connection to the front. The back was Tommy's more private playing area, and he proceeded immediately to a sharp slope at the lowest end of the yard where a small tree grew at the property's edge.

In his imagination the tree was Elfland. He sat on its mossy roots, trying to conjure the familiar reverie of elf-voices calling to each other among the leaves. But it was all very dim now; much stronger was the presence of his mother and Jesus watching from the sky.

"Dear Jesus," he prayed. "Please forgive me for hitting that boy. Please forgive me. I'll do everything I can to make up for it. I didn't mean to do it. I hope he's all right. Please make sure he's all right. Please help him. And please please forgive me. I'll try to be good. Amen."

He ended the prayer there, before adding a postscript that he suspected might be futile. "And please," he asked, "Please bring my Mommy back."

Chapter Three

After the foreign boys left, the Indian returned to his boulder and sat staring at where the eastern path went over the edge of the plateau. The pain in his cheek, which began as a sharp sting, dulled gradually into a throbbing ache. He tried touching the wound a few times, but this made it sting again, and after awhile he gave up and sat miserably with his right cheek feeling three times heavier than his left. After forty-five minutes he lost the energy to cry and was reduced to waving away flies when they landed on the edge of the wound. In this he wasn't much different from the sheep, which, bound at their hind legs, tripped over occasionally and were scored with small cuts. Insects plagued their lives.

The boy's name was Chaco. He was the eldest of five children in a miserably poor family that lived on the edge of a ravine. His duty as the most responsible child was to watch over the family's small flock of sheep; he escorted them with his father to the plateau every morning, and waited until evening for his father to return.

The hours passed more slowly than usual, for in addition to the customary boredom, he now had to endure the ache in his cheek, the flies, and the humiliation of being attacked by two strange boys. Yet for one of the few times in his life he felt some sympathy for the animals he was watching. He did not pity them, but felt a degree of companionship with them since they were around during the attack and were the only creatures that could salve his loneliness.

Chaco wondered again and again why the blond gods attacked him, and when his position on the boulder became uncomfortable he shifted ever so slightly so that the movement wouldn't cause his cheek to ache more. The flies pestered him mercilessly.

The clouds floated through the blue sky with serene detachment. Every so often a breeze came over the plateau, rustling the dry grass, and occasioning a low murmur among the sheep. It was beautiful weather, yet the fitfulness of the wind, and the stillness of the plateau between gusts, gave the place an atmosphere of harsh austerity. As the sun began falling in late afternoon the sky became gray, and Chaco felt even worse. He made an appeal to the Father, the Son, and the Blessed Mother above him.

"Please send my Papi here early. Please don't make me sit here. Please send my Papi early so I can leave. Please send me a doctor. And please make the pain go away."

He finished the prayer and crossed himself, feeling an acute relief that someone had listened to him. But his prayer was greeted by the patient mystery that greets all prayers, and by the empty sky that made him feel so alone.

In the early evening, as the sun descended over the range of mountains west of the city, the boy's father appeared at the accustomed time. He came from the direction of the dying light on a different path than the rich boys had taken, accompanied by the family dog. The dog was an energetic little mongrel that ran from one side of his master to the other, as if trying to raise the man's enthusiasm by example. But the animal was ignored, and Chaco's father advanced with slow, regular steps. He looked tired. His brown, wide-brimmed hat seemed heavy on him, and he was slightly bent over. He wore his black hair in a single long braid down the back of his poncho. The looseness of the poncho and the width of his hat over his skeletal frame gave him an appearance of lightness and fragility: a gust might take him, but he proceeded anyway with a resigned sense of purpose. He lifted an arm languidly as a greeting to his child.

When Chaco caught sight of his father his feeling of humiliation, which had dulled into a general feeling of hopelessness, revived as he relived the memory of the attack. He finally had an audience besides the sheep. The boy began crying freely, and watched his father with love and gratitude as he approached the rocks. For many hours he had understood that the one advantage of having the wound was that he would be pampered all evening and shown the attention his parents usually spared for the youngest kids. He had been relishing the idea all afternoon.

"What happens now? What happens now?" exclaimed his father sharply. He had been startled out of his thoughts, and his first reaction was to observe that the boy was blubbering and needed discipline.

"Two gringos, Papi! They came and shouted dirty names at me, and they cut my cheek!"

"Gringos? Let me see." The countenance of his face softened, and when he saw the gash in the cheek surrounded by watery fluid and dry blood, he felt his chest contract. He put an arm around his son, and lifted his poncho to wipe the wound. The wool was filthy.

"Ay, Papi! It hurts!"

"What happens now, little man? Did they hurt my boy? There it goes, there it goes. Ay, ay, there it goes." He waited until the boy stopped crying. "They did you a nasty one, ay, yes, they did you a nasty one, Chaquito. How does it seem now, eh? How does it seem?"

"All right, Papi."

"They did you a nasty one, eh?"

"Yes, Papi. They yelled dirty names at me, and they threw rocks at me, and—they ran away. Ran away!"

"They ran away. Gringos. Ay." Señor Achuale put his other arm around his son and held him, even as he reproached himself for not protecting the boy. His usual methods with his children were quite stern. He had a desperate feeling that they wouldn't get by unless they were tough, and he wasn't terribly patient besides. But when he was moved deeply by something his prickly shell gave way to a reserve of tenderness. It was such a moment that Chaco had waited for all afternoon, and he wasn't disappointed.

"Did you see where they came from, Chaquito?"

"From there—the path to the houses."

"Did you recognize them, Chaco? Do you know which house they came from?"

"No, Papi. I don't know."

Señor Achuale did not communicate the bitterness he felt at the reply, or the inadequacy he felt as a poor man. It was certain he could do nothing to catch the gringos, and doubtful it would mean anything to find them. The size of the gash on the boy's cheek meant he would have to pay for a visit to a doctor to sew it up. And a visit to the doctor meant—money: pieces of silver, skinned off the family's budget for tomatoes and onions, going into the doctor's palm month after month. But there was no way around it: the boy had to go to the doctor. Already the coins, with their torturous little weights, slipped away from him in his imagination to the waiting hand. And why would rich foreign children pick on his boy, who could do them no harm, and meant nothing to them?

"You don't know which of the houses they came from?" he tried again.

"No Papi. I've only seen them up here. They've come up before and watched me. They've watched me, but I don't know where they came from."

"Ay, ay." Replied the father gruffly. "They ran away."

He gently lifted Chaco off the boulder and stood him on the grass. Then he patted him: but a sharp restlessness came into Señor Achuale's eyes that put the boy on guard.

The Indian left his son leaning against the rock, and set about untying the bound legs of the sheep for their evening march back to the pen. The mongrel suddenly found a role for himself, and began barking with officious snaps at the newly freed sheep. There was no hostility in the dog's barks, and the sheep took it as a kind of play-acting that was safe to ignore. There were already relieved murmurings of "Maaaa!" among those that were able to move their knees, although Achuale had been none too gentle with them. He expressed his frustration by jerking at the bound legs of the animals before untying each rope, then pushing the sheep away with contempt. He eyed them as if they were on the verge of mutiny, keeping his bitter dark glances away from his son. To Chaco it was a real luxury not to help with the last chore of unbinding the sheep; and he watched his father with gratitude.

"And the gringos, did they throw things at the sheep as well?" asked Señor Achuale as he tugged at another leg. "Did they hurt the sheep?"

"No, Papi, they just threw rocks at me."

Señor Achuale said nothing. His son's answer disturbed him a great deal. Something about how his child had been singled out, and how the foreigners had watched him before, gave the attack a viciousness he couldn't understand. Deliberate cruelty to animals he was aware of and could at least fathom. But the gringos had left the sheep alone: he couldn't understand what motive would impel wealthy children with no problems of their own to prey on his own unfortunate boy. What meanness brought them out of their beautiful walled homes to throw rocks at an Indian on the plateau?

After a few minutes the sheep were untied, and Señor Achuale gathered the lengths of rope and put them over his shoulder. The animals were glad of their freedom and spread out into the field with halting steps as they tested their hind legs. The dog ran along the edge of the flock, yapping like a master of ceremonies. Achuale walked over to the boulder where the boy had been sitting all afternoon and picked up a long stave leaning against it. Then he patted the boy on the shoulder and signaled that it was time to go. He didn't expect Chaco to help keep the sheep together, and so did twice his usual work, running from one side of the flock to the other, forming it into a line with cries of "Hui!... Hoo!" and a few waves of his staff. The sheep were quite familiar with the staff and did their utmost to avoid it. Even the dog seemed in awe of his master, fired up with the quality the mongrel admired most—enthusiasm.

"Hoo!"

Father and son, with the animals before them, came to the edge of the plateau and descended the path to the construction sites and the rich neighborhood below. Their progress was slower than usual: Achuale didn't want to hurry the boy and make the throb in his cheek worse. They nodded at Manuel as they came in sight of the paved road, and the father made a note to ask him directions to the houses of the two blond boys.

On the way downhill they passed the houses in the highest and wealthiest neighborhood, and Achuale speculated bitterly on the lives within their walls. His mood wasn't eased by the quality of the sunset; if anything, he reacted against it. There was a beautiful softness in the range of blues and pinks and violets above the opposite range of mountains. The colors seemed to imply that there really is no harshness in the world, no injustice: have patience and watch me. Achuale looked away, and with restless black eyes that he tried to hide from his son, monitored the flock.

Two-thirds of the way down the mountain they turned into a dirt road, which, like so many projects begun by the government or developers, started abruptly and ended nowhere. After a couple hundred yards the road withered into a dirt path that wound along the side of the slope and passed through suicidally steep cornfields. The sheep negotiated the path casually, urged on by the irrepressible dog. As darkness fell, they came upon a ridge with six shacks emitting the glow of candlelight. Chaco was very pleased to see his house among them, and relished the thought of the fuss that would be made over his wound.

Achuale let his son walk ahead to the nearest of the shacks, and directed the sheep into a pen with the usual "Hui's!" and "Hoo's!" while whacking the ground with his staff. Then he closed the gate to the pen and leaned against it. The pen had a fence of tied sticks, branches and stalks, and looked as precarious as the shacks and cornfields around it seemed to be. Achuale listened to the cries of dismay that greeted the boy and the rustling of his family inside the shack. The dog had stayed outside, and after trying to decipher his master, gave up and lay down in the dirt. Achuale was reflecting on the doctor's bill and one more debt he would be a slave to. He could practically feel the coins balancing in his mind.

Well after his family began wondering what was keeping him, Achuale trudged up to the shack and was blocked at the entrance by the figure of his wife. "No shame! What are these people?" she railed at him. "Came here and hit our boy! As God is in the sky, they're devils—devils! These gringos—shameless!" Florencia was a large woman, with a brown skirt and a loose red sweater that exaggerated the fullness of her body. With her youngest baby slung on her back she looked massive and undefined. Only her round expressive face went against this impression: it was still pretty and extraordinarily sensitive to her moods.

"They ran away," said Achuale with a resigned voice that infuriated her.

"They ran away! Well, they'll pay for it, that's what! God didn't put the rich on earth so they could crawl into little holes. Cowards! Pure cowards, nothing more! They'll pay, I'm telling you that!"

"What are you talking about, woman? Get me some food and wash his face."

Achuale settled onto a tiny stool that would have fit a four-year-old comfortably. He looked about the room with a disgruntled expression, but the bristly exterior that his family watched so attentively dampened a bit, and he looked over at the boy with a kind of patient worry.

"How is that hurt feeling now, eh, boy?"

Except for the brief altercation between his parents, the situation had lived up to all of Chaco's expectations. He hadn't been pampered so much since the baby was born. The wound fascinated his twin younger brothers, and his sister Sylvia, who adored him, treated him like a hero.

"Oooh, it's a really ugly cut Chaquito," she said admiringly. "The skin is really wide apart, and there's so much blood, and there's this oozy stuff all around it!"

Chaco described again how big the rock was, and as he recalled the incident the two boys became somewhat less mysterious. Something about repeating the story simplified the situation in his mind, so that the awful question of the boys' motives became less important than it was when the rock was actually thrown. His attitude toward the boys hardened until they became in his mind what they were in the telling: representatives of their class. He was glad now that he'd been attacked by gringos instead of Indian kids—it made the wound that much more prestigious.

Chaco's mother used a wet cloth to wipe the edges of the wound with a dabbing motion, making a fuss over the boy. Then she served her husband a plate of lima beans with stale bread and passed portions to her children. She looked as if she wanted to accuse Achuale of something, and yet was quite ready to forgive him—she was that angry, and that generous. Her face registered a barely contained anxiety, and she served dinner with the formal manner of a nurse.

"It's going to get infected without a doctor," said her husband matter-of-factly. "I'm taking him to the doctor to get it sewn. Get us some coffee."

"An infection!" sighed Sylvia with awe. "Chaquito is going to be infected!" The novelty of the situation was too much for her, and the sprite of a girl went outside to tell her neighbors. The dog, alert to any excitement, pricked up his ears and dashed after her.

"They're going to pay, they're going to pay, listen to what I'm telling you!" insisted Florencia.

"What are you telling me?" replied Achuale ironically. "That the gringos are going to pay for this doctor's visit? Maybe. They ran away. The guards in those shells near the top may have seen something; I don't know. Maybe I'll go up into the rich neighborhood and search it from house to house. Hah! Maybe I'll find the boys who did it. Maybe I'll tell that house what the boys did, and they will decide to pay for the treatment. And maybe," he added quietly, "they will decide not to."

When the boy and his father left the shack a few minutes later, Sylvia and a band of kids from the nearby shacks accompanied them. They followed for about a hundred yards. Then, as if they had reached a border of some kind, they stopped where the path met the dirt road, and waved goodbye. The last to leave was the little girl. She lingered for a while watching them, and said, "Good bye, Chaquito! May it go well, Chaquito!" Then, with one of her sudden impulses, she immediately ran all the way home, to the great delight of the dog.

The full moon illuminated the cornfields with a silvery light that glowed on the ripe stalks. The light was reassuring, and appeared to cast the crops, and shacks, and pens, under a cool and sympathetic intelligence. It seemed to say that the precariousness of the place was an illusion; that everything was really very solid, everything was very real. Chaco held his father's hand. The sending off by the children and the clasp of his father's hand made him feel cared for, and even secure; a feeling he had rarely experienced since being put in charge of the sheep. Even the wound didn't seem so bad, considering the wonderful things that were happening because of it.

"So you're feeling all right, eh? You can walk?" asked Achuale as they hit the paved road.

"I'm okay, Papi."

They made a left on the Avenida Bolivar and started walking downhill. The road followed the contours of the mountain, and for the most part the descent was gentle. But the hardness of the pavement made the reverberation of each step a little harder to take, and the throb in the wound became worse.

The boy distracted himself by making a game of dodging the cow-pies on the sidewalk, which gave off a rather pleasant smell. Then the slope began leveling off as they reached the skirt of the mountain. Smaller paved streets began intersecting with the avenida, and they arrived in a more crowded neighborhood. The view became less spectacular as they descended closer to the main part of Quito, and with the deteriorating view came a more modest quality of life. They were now in a simple middle-class neighborhood of concrete-block houses and small yards. Each house still had its own walls, however; the idea of looking like a fortress reflecting aspirations to be part of the neighborhood higher up, and affect a similar distrust of the poor. The walls were topped with broken glass.

After pausing at a few corners, Achuale turned into a narrow street named El Cid. The street must have been named after the illustrious knight flippantly, or out of some hope that it would one day develop into a place worthy of the legend; for there was nothing heroic about El Cid at all. A few cramped houses were clustered near the intersection, then the street dropped steeply and leveled off. At that point it led through a few isolated homes surrounded by vacant lots. One stood out for the simple reason that a street lamp was beside it; and to this house Achuale took his son. It was near the end of the block. Overgrown lots on either side gave the place an abandoned look, but there were lights inside and a television aerial on the roof. The aerial and the expansive yard were the only signs that this house was relatively more affluent than its neighbors; otherwise it had the same look of shabby respectability.

A plaque by the buzzer at the front gate announced to any passers-by that the house contained a medical office operated by Adolfo Mendez, MD. Achuale rang the bell, and for the first time since he left the shack, let go of his son's hand. He took off his hat, held it in front of him with both hands, and bowed his head in a gesture of respect.

Through the windows they saw shadows moving in response to the buzzer. Then the front door opened hesitantly.

"Well?" The voice belonged to a middle-aged woman.

"Good evening, Señora," Achuale called down the walkway. "Please excuse us for disturbing you. We have come because we need the attention of the doctor, Señora. Please excuse us." Achuale fixed his eyes steadily on the ground. His voice possessed the careful dignity of a servant. "My son was attacked and his face was hurt badly. He needs the attention of the doctor. If you would be so kind to ask the doctor to see him, Señora, we would be very grateful to you. Please excuse us for disturbing you this evening."

The woman said nothing, but advanced through the front door and down the steps, and approached the gate with a wary curiosity. Despite the drabness of her clothes and unkempt hair she walked with considerable poise. She was wearing sandals. When she arrived at the gate she looked at the Indians with a ruffled superiority that did not obscure her underlying kindness.

"Yes?" she asked in a more trusting, though peremptory, tone.

"It's my son, Señora. Some gringos attacked him. They hit him with a rock. They hurt his cheek very badly, Señora. We have come to ask for the attention of the doctor, if you would be so kind."

Chaco marveled at his father's manner. For a man who was usually so brusque and out of temper, he now displayed an extraordinary courtesy, as he did toward anyone of a higher station. It was necessary perhaps, but showed such a degree of dignity and refinement that the boy's admiration for his father swelled.

The woman opened the gate.

She bent over to look at Chaco with an air of authority, but when she caught a good glimpse of the wound under the light of the street lamp, her expression changed dramatically. A wave of pain passed over her face, followed by an almost inexplicable look of shame. She brought a hand to her mouth and stepped back.

"Well! Yes! Enter—come in! Enter," she commanded, as she made way for them. "Wait here a moment, please. No." She hesitated and put her hand on the boy's shoulder. It was an extraordinary thing to do. It was the first time that a woman not of Chaco's class had ever touched him. "No," she said in a flustered voice. "Better if you go directly to the office. There." She pointed to the garage, which was adorned, like the gate, with a plaque bearing the doctor's credentials. "I'll go fetch my husband."

She went back inside, and Chaco and his father walked over to the garage. As they waited there a lamp switched on, illuminating the driveway, and immediately attracting a swarm of moths.

Once inside Señora Mendez couldn't help smelling the hand with which she had touched the boy. She made her way down a dimly lit corridor to the living room, where her husband was sitting on the sofa. He was down to his undershirt, nursing a bourbon as he cackled at a soap opera. It was a Mexican series, which had long been his favorite, about a beautiful village girl who made her way to the capital and became a maid. She worked for a rather dissolute household, through which various wealthy men passed, usually in need of a moral lesson. They invariably fell in love with her, but after five years on the air she was still a virgin. Dr. Mendez had convinced himself that he watched the show to humor his wife; the fact that she usually busied herself in the kitchen after dinner, glancing only intermittently at the TV, didn't faze his conception. He kept her apprised of the plots, and was proud of the ironical attitude he cultivated toward the story.

"I think she's going to keep her virtue, Lucita," the doctor announced as his wife entered the room. He didn't turn to look at her. "The composer wants to make her a singer, but he also wants to—make her. Ha ha ha! I think she's too good for him, however. It's a pity, you know? I think she could use some, myself. These plots—they love making the poor so damn virtuous."

"It was a man and his boy outside," replied his wife with a touch of reproach. "The boy cut his cheek. It's very bad. I told them to go to the office. They're cholos," she added, with some hesitation. She was looking steadily at the glass of bourbon, but did not comment on it.

"Indians, eh? Well." He collected himself, running a hand through his hair. As he placed the bourbon on the coffee table the ice clinked. The glass was nearly empty. "Well—go let them in. Please. I'll be there directly." He stood up, feeling slightly woozy, and ran his hand through his hair again. His face took on a serious, concentrated look more in keeping with his gray hair and carefully clipped mustache; and the sudden decisiveness of his manner was pleasing to his wife. But a common thought passed between them: it was about the bourbon. The doctor wondered whether he had had two or three. Anyhow it couldn't be helped.

"Go, go," he commanded his wife reassuringly. Señora Mendez looked at him a bit skeptically but obeyed.

"Indians, Indians," muttered the doctor under his breath. "So be it." He went to the kitchen, where the maid was washing dishes, and ordered a cup of coffee. Then he went to the bathroom, washed his face and hands, and put on a white coat over his T-shirt.

The arrival of his new patient affected him in an elevating way. It called to mind the honor of his profession, and when it came to its most humane aspirations, Dr. Mendez liked to consider himself exemplary. He never turned away the sick. Yet his career had not gone particularly well, and whereas many of his classmates had gone on to wealthy neighborhoods and a well-off clientele, his patients came to him because—they could not afford a more expensive doctor. It came to that. Dr. Mendez liked to believe that the wealthy avoided him because of a stigma attached to dealing so often with the poor: it lent credence to his idea that there was an unappreciated, noble strain in his character, and that he had made sacrifices to keep his integrity. He only rarely admitted that his methods were not up to date, that he was lazy, and that he drank. In the destitute neighborhoods close to his own, and on the steep mountains where the Indians eked out an existence, he was known as the doctor who was always available. Not as a particularly compassionate doctor, nor as a particularly skillful one, but as a doctor who never closed his door to the poor. That was why two Indians from a hamlet he had never visited interrupted his ritual in front of the television. Even now he decided that they might not be able to pay for his services, and was calculating the very cheapest way he could treat the boy without doing him any harm.

When he arrived at the office his wife had already put the boy on the examination table, and was busy collecting the implements necessary for treatment. Señor Achuale was sitting on a simple metal chair by the doorway on the side of the garage. He was leaning forward with an air of intensity and avoided looking anyone in the face. Dr. Mendez wondered at the queer way the Indians still dressed, and at the braid running down Achuale's back.

A single fluorescent tube illuminated the room, casting everything in a ghastly, dreary light, and couldn't have done more to emphasize the neglected appearance of the furnishings inside. In a glass cabinet above the sink there was a row of medical journals published in Madrid; but they were yellowed, and the most recent issue was twenty years old. They occupied the same distant past as the diploma on the wall above the boy.

"Well—let us have a look here. Let us see here," said the doctor with affable aloofness. "Ah, Lucita, bring me my glasses, will you?"

He turned on a lamp over Chaco, and without saying anything to the boy raised the head of the examination table. Then he put on his glasses and peered at the wound. The rock had left a jagged cut, much of which had become a conglomeration of dried blood and dirt. It would require at least fifteen stitches. Even with the detachment he cultivated, Dr. Mendez felt pity for the boy, although that pity was mixed with his usual distaste for Indians and disgust with the boy's smell.

"His face was wiped before he came here, no?" asked the doctor.

"His mother wiped his cheek. Yes," said Achuale.

"The wound is still dirty enough. How long ago did this happen?"

"In the afternoon, on top of the mountain. He was watching our sheep. Some gringo boys attacked him. Hours ago."

"Yes," said Chaco. He looked into the doctor's eyes, and was met by a disinterested, professional expression.

"Well," said Dr. Mendez lightly. "It was certainly strong of you to hold out all this time. You're a strong, strong boy."

He retreated to the counter where his wife had laid out a tray with green soap, some cotton swabs, and a bowl of warm water, and brought them over to the boy. Then he began cleaning around the cut with short dabs that always seemed to be less delicate than he intended them to be.

"Ay!" exclaimed the boy repeatedly.

"That's all right. I'm just cleaning. This part won't take very long at all. There—"

"Ay!"

"A little patience..." drew out the doctor with a few more dabs.

After another "Ay!" Dr. Mendez decided he had touched the wound a little too hard. He was nervous about his hands. He walked back to the counter with the tray, the fear in the boy's eyes fresh in his mind. Señora Mendez, with deft, efficient movements, had gathered the implements for stitching and set them on the counter for her husband to collect. She gave him a look that carried an odd combination of sympathy and suspicion. Again a thought passed between them about the bourbon.

The doctor picked up the needle, some silk thread, and a gauze pad, handling them with unusual care to prove that his hands were up to the task. His handling was so fine and deliberate that he felt quite pleased with himself. His sense of nobility buoyed him up, and with it came resentment at the extent to which he was unappreciated. Here he was, dealing with another patient who couldn't pay. His resentment tended to make him cheap, and he decided, with a great deal of compassion for the poor boy, that he simply couldn't afford to waste any anesthetic on him. The boy would live through it anyway, and Dr. Mendez consoled himself with a line he had never forgotten from the Bible: "The poor will always be with us."

His wife wasn't blind to the fact that he had not picked up one of the items she had laid out, and she followed him to the examination table whispering, "And the anesthetic? The anesthetic?"

"Oh, no, no, no," replied Dr. Mendez in a very even voice. "The cut is too close to the eye. Too dangerous."

It was such a bold, confident lie that the doctor was proud of the way he had asserted authority over his wife. He adjusted his glasses; bent over the boy in a probing, sympathetic manner, and said: "The gringos did this to you, eh? The gringos?" There was a curious edge to the doctor's voice, an anger that moved the boy deeply. He didn't know that the doctor resented gringos because they had never been his patients, a grievance that fed a desultory nationalism.

"Yes, Doctor," replied Chaco. From that moment the look of the doctor's face, with its slightly desiccated skin and gray bristles, the gray eyes magnified under the glasses, and the unpleasant alcohol-scented breath, reminded him of the word "gringo"; just as he remembered the blond god with the rock as the needle made its first pinch into his skin.

"Ayyy!" gasped the boy.

Gringo.

"Now, now, it still has to come through the other side.

There."

"Ahhh!"

"One," said the doctor with some satisfaction. "Just fourteen more, little señor. You have to be brave. It'll be over soon."

"Ahhh!"

"Two," counted Dr. Mendez. Tears were coming to the boy's eyes, and the doctor found the look of terror in them a bit unnerving. "Three."

"Ahhh!"

Gringo.

The sense of adventure and pride with which Chaco had seen the visit had now evaporated. There was something about the doctor he didn't trust, and with each of the terrible clumsy pinches he thought of the blond boy, with his look of superiority, holding the rock. The treatment was far worse than getting cut in the first place, and he looked for his father desperately. He didn't understand the rigid way Achuale was sitting in the chair.

Gringo. Gringo. Gringo.

"Ay, Papi! Please, please stop! It hurts hurts hurts hurts!"

"You could have!" admonished Señora Mendez under her breath. Though the boy didn't realize it, she was behind him stroking his hair. The doctor ignored her. He knew well enough there would be domestic troubles once the cholos left. He made another puncture into the skin.

The boy screamed.

"Ah—can't be helped," said the doctor nervously. He began to wish he had used the anesthetic after all, cost or no cost. There was something wrong with his hands, and he admitted it was the bourbon, but it was too late—he was halfway done. Besides, he had already made an excuse. He pulled at the thread and made another prick.

Gringo.

"Ahhh!"

"Damn. Please come here and hold your son," said the doctor gruffly. He looked at Achuale with an accusing air. "His feet."

The Indian got up and did as he was told. "What happens now? What happens now?" he said tenderly to his son.

There were five more stitches to do. It was unfortunate for the doctor that he had to treat a wound in the boy's face instead of his back; it subjected him to the dark pool of the boy's eyes each time he bent over to make a suture. It didn't help either that his skin was so young and smooth: he knew the face of the child would be marred for life, thanks to the clumsiness of his fingers under the influence of the bourbon. But it couldn't be helped now. Even the boy's rotten teeth depressed him and he wondered, with his usual mixture of sympathy and distaste, what possible future the boy could expect. "There will always be the poor." He reminded himself of that, but avoided looking at his wife, knowing that her reproach would dispel any complacency that all was in God's hands.

Gringo. Gringo. Gringo.

"Two more to go," said Dr. Mendez affably.

By this time Chaco had lost the energy to scream, and responded to the last sutures with dazed grunts. He thought "gringo" each time the needle entered his skin, "gringo" each time it came out the other side of the cut. It was the only word that could concentrate his mind.

"Well," said the doctor with a last pull of the thread, "it looks like we're finished."

Chaco gradually became aware that the soothing fingers of the doctor's wife were running through his hair. He felt more puzzled by her kindness than grateful. His father was watching him with his hat in his hands. Already the doctor was regaining his self-confidence, as he wiped the last smears of blood from the edge of the stitching. Now that it was over he convinced himself that the whole thing had mostly been handled rather well—under the circumstances.

The doctor helped the boy down from the examination table and gave him an aspirin. Señora Mendez stood behind Chaco for a moment with her hands on his shoulders, then went to a drawer and returned with two lollipops. Lollipops! The generosity was unbelievable. Chaco looked at the woman with awe and would have smiled at her, but his cheek hurt very badly, and she wore an unusual heavy expression he didn't understand. Her face was sagging with shame.

"How much do I owe you, Doctor?" asked Achuale, with his head bent over the hat he was clutching. "We are very grateful for your services. It was very kind of you to help us this evening." He made a pretense of not acknowledging his son or noticing that anything had gone wrong.

"Ah, sixty sucres, Señor...ah..." He had not asked the Indian's name, and decided to dispense with the question now. "Sixty, but that is for the materials only. The services are free—that is my pleasure." He gave Achuale a correct but magnanimous smile, and patted the boy on the shoulder, with a slight pressure toward the door. "Yes, yes, yes. Well. Pay when you can, there is no hurry. When you can. Will you open the door, Lucita? Come back in two weeks—say, Wednesday, September 15th—to have the stitches out."

The Indians passed outside and said goodnight. Dr. Mendez was steeling himself for the confrontation with his wife, who glared at him once the door was shut. He regretted not using the anesthetic, but thought again that *there will always be the poor*. Surely, he thought philosophically; surely, he thought with a particular emphasis on the boy, there is a reason the poor suffer more than most.

At first Chaco clutched his father with one hand, and his prized lollipops with the other. The pain in his cheek was so bad, however, that he began whining only a few feet from the office. Rather than scolding him, as he normally would, his father simply picked him up and let him ride on his shoulders.

Achuale was thinking about the sixty sucres, subtracting vegetables from his family's diet so that he could pay the doctor's bill by the time the stitches were removed. He was very depressed. He thought only vaguely of finding the house where the blond boy lived. He had learned to accept things for what they are.

Achuale did not consider what was going on in his child's mind, and would have been surprised at the complexity of the boy's response to the events of the day. Along with the terrible pain in his face, Chaco felt exhilaration at having survived the ordeals and being singled out for them. He did not understand why all of it had happened, and the experiences left a variable impression on him. The memory of the gods approaching from the edge of the plateau mingled with the loneliness that followed his humiliation, and then the welcome given to him by his family and neighbors. The kindness of the doctor's wife and the gift of the lollipops even mitigated the agony of being sewn up. It was the last time in his childhood he was to ride on his father's shoulders, and that privilege was one of the extraordinary things that gave his experience a tingling mixture of injury and pride. In that frame of mind he was carried by his father past the scattered houses of El Cid, and up the slope to the Avenida Bolivar, where they ascended the mountain under the moonlight and the stars.

Chapter Four

In the years since his mother's death Tommy's prayers had become very elaborate. He prayed several times a day, very informally, whenever he encountered something that could use the intervention of God. To someone else the situation might seem trivial. Once he swatted a fly on the windowsill of his bedroom, and when it occurred to him that other flies might be bent on revenge for the act (especially the Fly King), he prayed for the insect's recovery. But God, after hearing the supplication, didn't lift a finger for the fly, and that was that.

Tommy never accepted that his mother was dead. Perhaps, with his belief in the kindness of Jesus, he didn't believe in death at all. He often prayed for a visit from his mother; just as often he prayed that his stepmother would avoid him or not discover some infraction. She was a merciless punisher. When he heard her whipping his brothers or screaming at his sister he prayed that lightning from Heaven would strike her down. But again, Jesus did nothing but observe, saving his retribution till Judgment Day.

Nor had prayer saved Tommy from the torment he inflicted on himself after his crime against the shepherd boy. Sometimes it felt like he had thrown the rock at himself, for the impact cleaved his mind. During the days following the attack he lived in constant fear of discovery and hid in his room for hours after school, pretending to study. He only ventured outside briefly before dinner, and only to the back, where there was no chance of being spied from the Avenida Bolivar as the Indian urged his flock downhill. But as he sat in the sweet-smelling grass, he was tortured by Jesus' mercy, and sought out the German shepherd or a cat, to overwhelm them with affection.

By the weekend, to Tommy's surprise, no one had come to the house to accuse him. Relieved as he was, he prayed for the cholo's forgiveness, and began to perceive his adversary in a more sympathetic light. He identified the Indian with the shepherd boys in biblical stories, and began to feel toward him the same sentimental compassion he usually reserved for animals. Becoming a victim elevated the Indian considerably in Tommy's odd moral vision, and he fantasized about leaving gifts outside the boy's hut—wherever it was. But the probability of getting caught in the process was chilling.

He didn't have the courage to tell Geoffrey about his change of heart. At recess on Monday, when no one else was around, the Irish boy, still jaunty with victory, asked, "Has your step-mum found out yet?"

"Oh, no—not yet."

"I haven't told *anybody*. We really gave it to that bastard, didn't we?"

"We sure did," replied Tommy. "That—that son of a bitch!"

The secret became a bond of their friendship. It also constricted what they did together. In the afternoons they rode the bus from the Cotopaxi Academy until it dropped them off at the foot of the mountain where a tienda stood at the intersection with the avenida uphill. The boys walked up Bolivar, past the middle class district toward the grandeur of their own neighborhood. It was a twenty-minute walk, taken slowly. They discussed their teachers, victories over the rival gangs at school, and wars over the summer at the construction sites. Geoffrey realized that Tommy had not planned any wars recently, and the expeditions to the construction sites and the plateau had ceased altogether. The Irish boy understood his friend's fear of discovery, even if he didn't share it since he hadn't thrown the rock. But he never mentioned it as their friendship faded with the end of their adventures. Geoffrey's house was below his friend's, so they always reached it first: Tommy walked the last stretch alone, keenly aware that he would be spied if the shepherd boy passed at an unaccustomed time.

In the mornings, before breakfast, Tommy often gazed through the living room window as Chaco and his father turned off the avenida onto an old path, formed out of a gully, to the right of the front gate. It was the traditional route to the plateau, and avoided the twists and turns through the construction sites visible from the front yard to the left and above the house. In the days after the incident the father did most of the work herding the sheep uphill: the boy followed behind with a dazed look. Tommy wasn't close enough to see the wound on the boy's cheek, but knew it must look horrible, and watched with a pang of shame. But what could he do about it? He watched: torn between his conscience and fear of his stepmother, which was much more powerful.

After a few weeks the shepherd boy began coming up the mountain alone. He ran back and forth along the flock with the dog as if his new responsibility had given him an infusion of energy, keeping the animals in formation by whacking their legs with his staff. As far as Tommy could tell the sheep had never been treated so cruelly, and his memory of the attack on the Indian made the ongoing torture of the animals all the more wrenching to him. In the evening the cholo would return alone the same way, herding the animals with the same ruthless efficiency, as Tommy observed from a darkened window.

He felt lucky at least that his stepmother overlooked him most of the time. Her first pronouncement after she entered the family had been that the children needed more discipline. That was over a year ago. "Discipline was not one of your mother's forte's," she explained with an insinuating smile, "and it shows." Mr. Montavan, his expression preoccupied, agreed with everything that

Miriam said, as if the whole program had been discussed in detail after their wedding. So there was to be discipline. All four of the children, in a bewildered sort of way, agreed with the thesis because of a need to believe their father knew what was best for them. So Miriam taught them a song that would ease them into the reality of their new life:

Mourning days are over
So is the daily routine
Got-to stick to the subject
There's no ti-ime for play-ing!

Tommy often sang the song to himself, but it only reminded him of his mother. Discipline, as an end in itself, was not a comforting thing to live for, not nearly as comforting as kindness or a mother one could tell one's problems to. But Miriam apparently knew better. Her methods of discipline included the liberal use of several of her husband's belts, and for minor infractions of etiquette, the endless writing of a simple statement, such as: "I will not hold my knife with my left hand." This would be written five hundred times over, until the boy's wrist felt like falling off, and required several sharpenings of the pencil.

At first Richard, Tommy's eldest brother, had rebelled against the discipline and unfairness, but their father didn't back him up, and Richard was shown correct behavior with the belt. Soon Richard spent most of his time in his room; so did Katy, and Billy, who Tommy shared his room with. Tommy escaped outside. Often, while playing in one of the yards, he felt the presence of Miriam lurking somewhere in the house, and fear touched him like a shadow. Occasionally she even remembered him, and appeared on the deck next to the fountains.

"Tommy. Have you done your home work yet—all of it?"

"Yes, Miriam."

"All of it?"

"Yes, I did."

"Come inside and show me."

He would obey, leaving the security of his imaginary world behind, sometimes wondering whether discipline wasn't really the best thing for him, and whether Miriam really might be the kind of mother he deserved. At least, he now reminded himself, she had never found out about the shepherd boy.

Even so his private world contracted, and when he fantasized about journeys to other planets, or the world of the elves, or simply played with the dog, his adventures were confined to the flowerbeds and trees and slopes of the back yard. His remove to the back had a pleasant, if unintended effect on the cook: for Rafael was fond of the boy and observed him more often now from the kitchen window. The sight affected the cook the way most children did, with a hint of a promise and richness in life that had escaped him personally.

When the rainy season arrived in late October a shower-burst hit the mountain most afternoons at four and departed capriciously after twenty minutes, so that when Tommy ran to Elfland afterwards it was dewy with freshness. The altitude of the neighborhood put it in the vicinity of strange turns in the weather. Occasionally—sometimes once a week—a stream of frigid air met a thundercloud, and a shower of hail pelted the grounds. For a few minutes the yard was covered with white pellets, and Tommy, with his brothers and sister, ran outside to share in the exuberance of temporary winter and memories of home when their mother was alive. But the ice melted quickly, leaving the daisies and geraniums dominant in the flowerbeds. The extremes of weather and the extraordinary view of the city from the back yard contributed to the newly magical quality of the place, and Tommy's heart began to open up again.

The boy's most regular companion when playing outside was the gardener, who was the most mysterious of the servants. His name was Segundo. Unlike Rafael, he had never cut off his traditional Indian braid, and came to work wearing the wide brimmed cholo hat. He didn't live in the servants' quarters, though that choice was offered to him. No one was sure exactly where he did live, except that he had a family in one of the shantytowns within walking distance. Living away from the house gave him independence, and saved him from the humiliation of being under the constant surveillance of La Señora and sleeping next to the cat litter boxes. Perhaps for that very reason Tommy viewed him less condescendingly than the other servants and was a little in awe of him.

It wasn't necessary for the house to have a full-time gardener at all. But it wasn't necessary for the house to have the cook and his wife, and a houseboy, either. Servants were simply one of the accouterments that came with being a member of the Quito aristocracy, and Tommy, like everyone else in the family, accepted the fact. If there was a kitchen, someone must be hired to cook in it; if there were floors to be waxed, someone must be hired to do that job as well—meticulously and then over again. The work of the servants had very little to do with the comfort of the family, and everything to do with a heightened sense of style. The house the Aguillars built, and then abandoned so capriciously, had to be maintained at a furious pace to give it the atmosphere of easy luxury in which the children hid in their rooms.

The Aguillars had bequeathed some remarkable grounds to their tenants as well. While the other servants scrubbed the windows and drained and cleaned the long pool under the fountains on the deck, Segundo kept up the yard. He arrived early in the morning, and often went about his tasks all day without encountering the Señora at all. She did not have a whole lot to do with the grounds, and kept most of her intrigues confined to the house. Yet occasionally she met the gardener as he came in by the gate in the morning, and offered instructions on which flowerbed to weed that day.

"Yes; well—of course. That certainly makes sense, Señora," he would reply. "I was thinking that myself. That's where I will work today." He displayed an unflappable deference to everyone in the family, and held extraordinary reserves of dignity in his thin frame. His courtesy was a kind of lubricant that allowed him to go through life undisturbed. He never betrayed his thoughts, and rarely had anything to do with the other servants. He brought his own lunch to work, and ate in the shade of the dogwood tree at the bottom of the back slope.

Segundo rarely spoke to the boy, and his attitude toward him—as it seemed to be toward all things—was one of benevolent neutrality. He never seemed curious about the games of Tommy's imagination, and the boy had long ceased to be self-conscious about playing with his elf-doll or plastic soldiers in front of the Indian. They often behaved as though oblivious to one another, and as Tommy lived rapturously through adventures he thought up in Elfland, the gardener, a few feet away, mulched the flowerbeds that had been transformed so utterly in the boy's mind.

Over time Tommy came to realize how observant and considerate the gardener actually was. When the boy gathered sticks into a corral and left them in the flowers to form a barricade in some extraterrestrial war, Segundo did not disturb them. If the boy became fascinated by a growth of mushrooms along the dogwood's roots (he imagined them into an elf village), the gardener did not cut them down. Segundo worked for the perfection of the garden, yet he did not let it interfere with the world into which Tommy escaped. That tact and his mastery over the yard made him a very respectable figure in the boy's eyes.

If Tommy were ever to break the unspoken rules of their relationship, he might have asked Segundo why he favored daisies and geraniums over every other flower. Daisies and geraniums, everywhere! But it wasn't any use, any more than it made sense to wheedle out of the Indian where he kept his family, and why he ate alone and kept apart all the time. His privacy was bound up with his integrity, and Tommy knew better than to disturb the Indian's wall of tact.

The hold he came to exert over Tommy was remarkable, considering he never tried to influence him in any way. If he happened to remark, in his off-hand manner, "The humming-birds are out today, feeding on the flowers. Ah, yes, there they are!" it was enough to mystify the boy. Why would the gardener make such an obvious observation, or make an observation at all, considering he rarely spoke? What was his motive? The look on the Indian's face would remain as enigmatic as ever as he went to work trimming the grass against the wall. Tommy yearned for the gardener's approval, though he had no idea how Segundo would express it.

One afternoon the gardener remarked casually, "I don't see you playing in the front yard anymore."

What?! What did he mean by that? "No?" asked Tommy.

"Ah, well—no. I haven't seen you playing in the front for a long time."

For several days the boy mulled over what the Indian said. It was obvious that his strategy of staying away from the shepherd's view hadn't been as subtle as he thought, and yet he wasn't sure what Segundo meant—except that he wasn't playing in the front yard. Though the gardener hadn't changed his behavior toward him, queasiness came over Tommy that the game was up. But after a few days nothing happened, and he relaxed again.

"I've planted some flowers in the front. Some flowers—they're new. Would you like to see them?" asked the Indian a week later.

Again Tommy felt the shock of being discovered, but he detected no malice or calculation in the Indian. Was it really an act of friendliness? Why would the gardener suspect anything anyway? The boy followed Segundo reluctantly up the stone steps to the upper terrace. Along the part of fence with the best view uphill he found a bed of red geraniums, freshly watered, with droplets glowing on their petals. Once Tommy murmured his approval of the flowers, the Indian departed for the lower gardens again.

It was a long time since Tommy stood freely in the front, and the exposure was invigorating. He felt courageous: the view of the bend in the road leading up to the construction sites brought out his old enthusiasm for war games and his special destiny. It was too early for the shepherd boy to come down from the plateau, so Tommy lingered and revisited different sections of the yard that represented the intoxicating worlds where people lived in giant plants, visited moons in their cars, and never died.

The pattern of his life changed again in ways that only the gardener noticed, because only the gardener was paying attention. Tommy began spending more time in the front, playing by sections of the fence that allowed a view of the upper regions of the hill. He always left as the afternoon wore on, escaping to the back or to his room. Yet as the days went by he began testing himself, staying later and later in the afternoon, pretending he had nothing to hide. One Friday afternoon early November his courage did not desert him quickly enough and he faced the shepherd boy a second time.

It was growing dusky, the light withdrawing by degrees, draining the brilliance out of the garden. Tommy continued playing stubbornly: whether he'd forgotten the risk of staying in the open, or was ignoring it, even he couldn't say. The sight of sheep moving on the other side of the road lured his attention. The gray light suited them perfectly because the filth in their coats made them gray as well. They hardly bleated as they made the turn from the construction sites to the neighborhood of wealthy houses, and walked hesitantly, aware of freedom and restrained by fear. The animals mesmerized him, and it took a moment for Tommy to remember that the shepherd would be behind them. By then it was too late.

Chaco emerged from the path and stopped when he saw the gringo across the avenida. Yes! It was the little god who had struck him on the mountaintop months before! The blond boy was beyond the fence of a magnificent white house with windows reflecting the hillside and a row of fountains churning easily on the deck behind him. He was standing in a beautiful garden under the blue sky with the toy city below him. Chaco felt a chill as he realized how impregnable his tormentor was. He played with the word "gringo" in his mind as he remembered the attack on the plateau and the visit to the doctor. The gringo had given him the scar. He was standing there behind the fence, and he was safe.

The boys didn't communicate. They looked at each other with wondering expressions, enigmatic to one another. The stand off only broke when Tommy's magnificent German shepherd discovered there were outsiders on the other side of the road, and came charging brutally along the fence.

"Ar-Ar-Ar-Ar-Ar-Ar-Ar-Ar!"

To Chaco the violence underpinning the privilege of the gringo was very clear. He restrained his own dog, gripped his staff tightly, and with more than his usual harshness, threatened the sheep so that they walked more quickly. He was eager to tell his father he had discovered the house where the gringo lived.

Tommy watched him leave with an empty, powerless feeling. He knew that he had been found and that consequences, too terrible to consider, would follow.

"Oh please please please," he prayed fervently to Jesus. "Please don't let them do anything to me. Don't let Miriam touch me. Please!"

But Tommy's thoughts weren't entirely selfish at the moment, and he didn't want God to think they were, either. He finished the prayer by asking again that fortune visit the Indian boy and take his family away from poverty.

Chapter Five

ACHUALE WASN'T HAPPY WITH THE NEWS his son brought home. In the days after the incident, when he had gone from one construction site to another, none of the guards could tell him where the blond boys lived. In his heart he had been relieved. Now he had to confront the parents of the gringo kid, and as proud as he was, he knew that he would be dealing with them from a position of inferiority. His quest for compensation only placed him in his usual role as a supplicant to the rich—and was there any other role a poor man could take if he cared for his family? Achuale had a simple view of the situation and it melded well with a fatalistic attitude he had about being poor. He was born to that condition and he was sure that his children would remain in poverty as well. Hard work had done nothing to improve his life, and he'd long resented the Ladinos for keeping Indians like himself scratching to feed their kids. He accepted his lot because he could do nothing to change it, however, and believed strictly in a God of circumstances. It was quite at odds with the merciful deity the Spanish imposed after murdering their way to power, and Achuale often thought nostalgically about the banished Inca gods of the sun, the corn, and the weather, who were as volatile as the world itself. His heart and temperament would have made him an excellent pagan.

Unlike his father Chaco was flush with anticipation, and felt that justice for his wrong was imminent. That evening he described his second encounter with the gringo to all the children who would listen, and his stock among them rose substantially. "He lives in a palace—Ay! And he didn't say one word to me—nothing! And they have this big dog trained to kill people; it ran all along the fence barking like a firecracker. My papi and I, we're going up there in the morning to tell the parents of that house what he did to me. Hah! We'll see then!"

The morning came and Achuale was depressed. The chickens were already making a fitful racket, and there was nothing inviting about the gray light outside: the color always swept in at once, but only after the sun rose almost completely over the plateau atop the mountain later in the morning. In the evening, shadows from the opposite range of hills fell in the valley first, condemning the place to obscurity.

Achuale sat up from his wife's side without waking her, and stepped over the twins, who were sharing a mat on the floor. It would be minutes before the baby started crying. He went outside and stood there awhile for a few moments of privacy. Then he walked over to the pen where the sheep were kept and leaned over it. The animals moved toward him, expecting to be let out. But there was no one to take them to pasture if he and the boy went up to the rich neighborhood to make their claim: that was just one of the complications arising from the situation.

His family began stirring in the shack, and he heard his wife rebuking the twins sharply—she was like that in the morning. His moment of independence was over. He grabbed a bucket that was by the door, and made his way down a precarious path through the corn, with steps cut into the dirt, until he arrived at the stream at the bottom of the gully. He filled the bucket with water and climbed back up to his compound. Then he sat on one of the midget stools and watched his wife make coffee.

"Are we going soon, Papi? Are we going?" asked Chaco.

"Later. I have some errands to run first. It's early."

"Later? When?"

"Nine, maybe. Nine. They sleep late, those people."

"Nine!" said the boy incredulously. There was more than disappointment in the boy's voice; he was angry that his father was postponing his retribution. Achuale noticed how obvious the scar was when the boy's skin was stretched with emotion.

"No earlier than nine," repeated Achuale without apparent sympathy. He was training his boy to be hard.

The father left a disgruntled family behind as he went out to do his errands. He had arranged to work that day at a farm in the valley outside the city for twenty sucres; he had to walk there first and beg off work. It was a forty-five minute walk on a dirt road. When he arrived he approached the foreman with his hat held in front of him and his head bowed in the usual gesture of respect. The foreman was a fat man who considered most Indians devious and inscrutable; he listened to Achuale's excuse without pretending to believe it, and gave him leave with a snide smile of benevolence. It was a small victory for the Indian: the boss hadn't forbidden him to come back.

The loss of the twenty sucres rankled Achuale considerably. Then he remembered there was nothing to feed the sheep, and went off the road to an uncultivated slope and spent half an hour collecting grass with his machete. He stuffed the sweet-smelling stalks in a burlap sack and carried them the rest of the way home. It was an unusual risk, he thought: giving up a day's wages and keeping the sheep in their pen on the chance that a rich family would admit it had done something wrong. By the time he returned home the full force of the sun still hadn't reached the shack, but the opposite range of mountains and the city below were brilliant.

"Are we going now, Papi? Are we going now? Now?"

Again the father met Chaco with an unwaveringly hard expression: he ordered the boy to throw the grass into the pen, and went inside for another cup of coffee.

A few minutes later the two of them left the shack to make their claim. Chaco's sister followed them to the paved road with the dog, but the other children stayed behind this time, frightened by the bitter expression on Achuale's face—he wasn't one to encourage too much hopefulness in the young.

Chaco understood his father well enough to know there was a reason for his harshness, and he accepted it as part of his training. In the months since the incident on the plateau a subtle change had come over the boy. His face lost its wandering blank expression, replaced with a focused look that was sometimes cruel in its intensity. If a stranger glanced from Chaco's scar to his eyes, he might think the wound had altered the boy inside. But most of the time Chaco wasn't aware of the scar. His father had devolved more responsibility on him over the sheep, and it made him proud. He grew into his new role, and his harshness toward the sheep, now worse than ever, was a theatrical extension of the hardness he was fitting himself into. There was very little deliberate cruelty in the boy at all: he was simply indifferent to the sheep and manipulated them to earn his father's respect.

His two lollipops had lasted quite a while. The yellow one he had given to Sylvia; she hid it in her blouse and sucked it in a cornfield one day when the twins weren't around. Chaco saved the remaining one for a week and finally opened it one afternoon while he was with the sheep on the plateau. He was tempted to keep the wrapper as a souvenir, but on his second visit to the doctor, to remove the stitches, Señora Mendez gave him another. This one he kept for himself.

On the second visit Señora Mendez wasn't quite as friendly as before; she looked resigned and didn't say very much. The doctor, on the other hand, exuded a breezy confidence, and hadn't been drinking. He pulled the stitches out in a matter of minutes and Chaco only felt a number of sharp stings. This time the visit wasn't so bad, though he wondered why Señora Mendez flinched so when she saw him under the light. As they were leaving Achuale made the first of his payments to the doctor; two weeks later the Indian's family had gone without tomatoes and onions and the doctor was paid off. For some reason Achuale didn't let the boy come when he delivered the last bit of money, and Chaco wondered afterwards whether his father thought accepting lollipops from the doctor's wife was a sign of going soft.

It didn't take long for them to climb into the wealthy neighborhood. Chaco didn't feel as intimidated as usual by the houses; having a claim seemed to even the odds. But his father was still under the oppressive mood he had woken up to earlier and didn't speak to his son. Out of habit they walked on the undeveloped side of road, avoiding the cow-pies on the sidewalk. The properties on their left glimmered in the sunlight, with garden above terraced garden. The wild aspect of the slope to their right only made the rich houses seem even more exotic and luxurious, and the sense of ease and languor about them was spellbinding. In the fresh morning air, it seemed to Chaco that they were calling on Paradise, or least one of its local addresses.

"It's that house, Papi—that one! With the white walls and the black fence at the top of the road. With the fountains."

His father nodded, and Chaco thought he detected a flicker of doubt in his eyes, but it was hard to interpret, and anyway the boy was too enthusiastic to worry about it. Through the fence they saw a woman washing a window near the fountains.

"Listen to me. Listen to what I say. And only speak when I tell you. Well?"

"Yes, Papi."

"Do that. So this is the house," Achuale said morosely. "Well." He led his son across the street without showing any curiosity about the gringo residence at all: he mostly looked at the ground. When they arrived at the gate Achuale went through the transformation that Chaco found so mysterious. He took off his hat, held it to his chest in a profound gesture of respect, and bowed his head. Even the lines on his face seemed to ease, and he took on a bearing of such humility that the gesture announced, "I am your servant. Look at me and know that. I am your servant."

The servant raised an arm and pressed a buzzer under the name Aguillar. It was a little frightening to Chaco how his father's pride disappeared so quickly. The man stood there as if he expected nothing, and nothing was better than he deserved. He didn't deserve anything, because he was only a servant. A servant waits.

The buzzer had its usual effect. Rafael peered through the slit-shaped window in the kitchen, and when he saw two Indians at the gate a look of dismay came over his face. It was reserved but hostile.

A moment later the front door opened a crack and a portion of the cook's face appeared. The German shepherd barking behind him was obviously anxious to get to the gate. "Well?" asked Rafael.

"We are here to see the master of the house," replied Achuale calmly.

"What?"

"The master of the house. We have a matter to speak to him about." Achuale didn't make a special effort to be humble toward a servant who was simply another Indian like himself, but he was polite in an authoritative sort of way. Rafael looked him over with a resentful and embarrassed expression, and closed the door.

"What are they going to do, Papi? Are they coming back?"

"Quiet. Wait."

The door wedged open again. They could see the shadowy silhouette of a woman holding the knob inside; she was obviously listening to someone. Then she turned and opened the door all the way. She made no effort whatever to restrain the German shepherd, who lunged to the gate: it might as well have been household policy that he was to soften up any Indians importunate enough to ring.

"Ar-Ar-Ar-Ar-Ar-Ar-Ar-Ar!"

Chaco couldn't help stepping back, but his father, with an amazing display of self-discipline, remained where he was. The dog stuck his snout desperately through the railings trying to get his teeth into him.

The woman evaluated them a moment before approaching on the walkway, leaving the door open behind her. The cook watched briefly from inside before abandoning the situation to return to the kitchen. The woman had a pleasing, full-bodied figure just this side of voluptuousness. She walked with a casual, offhand lilt and seemed to know she was attractive. She carried a bored expression and seemed aware in an abstract way. Once she got closer, however, it was obvious that the expression conveyed an alert detachment that lent her a surprising air of authority. Her skirt and blouse were as casual as anything else about her: she was a person who took a lot for granted. Chaco noticed that she had a naturally pretty face, but there were traces of yesterday's make-up on it.

"Well," she said in Spanish that was surprisingly fluent. "You say you have business with this house. What is it?" Only now did she bother to restrain the dog, and when she commanded him to sit he obeyed immediately, licking his chops in a goofy sort of way.

"We have come to see the master of the house, Señora—please. We have a matter to discuss with him."

"Oh, yes? The 'master' of the house? And what about?" she asked ironically.

"The master, yes, Señora," replied Achuale, without realizing he had insulted her. "It is about my boy. A child of this house cut his cheek some months ago, Señora."

The woman looked down on Chaco with some interest, and made note of the scar. Unlike his father, the boy did not stand with his head bowed, and returned her look. He was still surprised at how pretty she was, though there was something disturbing about her. He couldn't detect any kindness in her, yet he was attracted to her in an odd way. Her eyes, for instance, were mesmerizing: they were a hazel brown of an almost indefinable shade, and only after staring at them to make sense of the color did one realize there was something shallow and glinting about them, like the copper bottom of a pan.

"Which child?" she demanded.

"A blond boy, about the height of my son." Achuale looked at Chaco for verification, and the boy nodded without taking his eyes off the woman.

"Very interesting," said Miriam matter-of-factly. To Achuale's surprise she didn't seem angry or insulted by the claim. Instead she seemed to find it agreeable; she was even a little smug about it. "I expect you will want to tell this to the 'master' of the house, no? I will get him. Then he will come out and you will repeat this information." She looked them over again and turned around. Once she was halfway to the door, the dog, feeling released from her command, went back to barking at the Indians. She made no gesture to stop him.

In his room Tommy heard the first ring of the doorbell with great foreboding. He was sitting at his desk pretending to read a book. When he heard Rafael say, "Indians at the door—I don't know what they want, Señora," he knew for certain he was doomed. From then on it was a matter of waiting to be discovered, and he listened to the agonizing footsteps of Miriam going to meet the visitors outside. He could scarcely imagine what his punishment would be or how long it would last. What bothered him just as much was the reaction of his father: Tommy couldn't bear the thought of falling in his eyes or losing any of his love. He leaned into the desk, resting his forehead in the open pages of the book, and prayed. Prayed for what? There was no chance now that he wouldn't be caught, and there was no one to rescue him. He prayed for mercy. The crisp sound of Miriam's shoes returned through the front door and turned into the den, where Tommy's father was.

"Well, there's some very interesting news outside, Peter. Indians. They want to speak to you."

"What, sweetheart?"

"There're a couple of Indians waiting for you outside. It's about your youngest son. They claim he cut the cheek of the boy out there. They want to speak to *you*." She studied him in a coolly insinuating way.

"Aw, shit. I mean, what is this? What the hell do they want?" Mr. Montovan looked up from his work with a pointed, harassed expression; his show of temper was meant to give him an air of ruffled authority.

"How am I supposed to know what they want? I'm not the 'master of the house.' They want to speak to you. You can handle it, I'm sure—no? Tommy's been up to something, I suspect."

"Shit. Saturday morning." He got up and stalked past his wife with an apparent lack of concern about her presence; in fact he was very aware that she had just crossed her arms and was taking a position on the matter.

He went outside. His countenance had softened considerably now that he was no longer in view of his wife, and he ordered the German shepherd to stop barking. The dog obeyed reluctantly, as if he considered it bad etiquette to shout orders from twenty feet away, and sat down with his ears erect.

The situation presented itself to Mr. Montovan gradually. He noted the humble stance of Mr. Achuale and the shy curiosity of the boy standing next him wearing the big hat. The subservience Achuale showed by holding his own hat to his chest in the hot sun was striking. Whatever his pride in the dog, Mr. Montovan felt ashamed that he had been allowed to bark at the Indians for so long.

"Good morning. And what's going on here?" he asked in a business-like way. His Spanish wasn't nearly as good as Miriam's. The Indians perceived him as a large man, more direct in manner than his wife, with a more open quality to his face. He was just as casually dressed.

"Good morning, Señor," replied Achuale. "I am sorry to disturb you on this day, but I have a matter to discuss with you, Señor. It is about my son. He was hurt some time ago by a young boy of this house, and since we did not know where he lived, we could not talk to you before. Yesterday as my son was returning home, he saw your boy in the front, and we knew which house he came from. That is why we came here to speak with you.

"Some time ago," continued Achuale, with the slow and steady speech he used when addressing superiors, "some months—my boy was watching our sheep on top of the hill. In the afternoon two boys—foreign boys with blond hair—came up on the plateau. One of them was your boy. They yelled bad words at him, Señor, dirty names. Then your boy—it was your boy, Señor—threw rocks at my son. One of the rocks hit his cheek and cut him badly. You see the scar, Señor. Then the boys ran away from what they'd done. Yes, Señor. They ran away. That is what we have come to tell you, Señor. We had to take the boy to a doctor. You can see that my boy had his cheek sewn up."

Achuale's manner was extraordinarily courteous; he never looked Mr. Montovan in the eye, and acted strictly as if he were paying the highest complements. The American quickly looked over to the boy. The wound had obviously been sewn very crudely. There was a crevice where the two sides of the cheek were joined; the boundary was a line of shiny gray skin. What a great pity, thought Mr. Montovan, that the boy hadn't gotten to a proper doctor.

"How do you know it was my son who did it?" he asked finally. There was something sharp in his tone, but he did not imply that the Indians were wrong.

"I saw him! I saw him!" replied Chaco immediately. "He was standing in the yard yesterday when I was going home. I saw him there! I remembered him."

"Chaco—quiet!" Achuale looked at him witheringly.

The expression on Mr. Montovan's face communicated a detached sympathy. "You look thirsty," he said. "Would you like some milk? How about something to drink?"

"Milk!"

It was too late. Achuale's inclination was to reject the offer politely; he wanted to keep to the business at hand, and was suspicious that the milk would make him indebted to the American. But since his son had already opened his mouth, he accepted in his slow, steady, formal manner.

Milk! Chaco could hardly believe his luck. His heart swelled, and he looked admiringly at the American. He decided that the foreigner was a fair man.

"Rafael! Rafael!" Mr. Montovan glanced at the slit-shaped window, and since he didn't get an immediate response, he stuck his hand through the gate, startling Achuale, and rang the bell. The dog was emboldened by his move and barked again.

"Quiet!"

The dog looked chastened.

Rafael appeared at the door rather haplessly and received instructions to bring two glasses of milk outside. He said, "Si, Señor," with the professionally neutral expression he assumed in questionable situations, and returned to the kitchen.

Mr. Montovan looked at the Indians a last time. Something about their manner made him believe them; he did not want to believe them. He felt sympathy for them and was a big-hearted man, but he wished they had not come to his house. He asked them to wait a few minutes while he talked to his son. Local conventions notwithstanding, Mr. Montovan was the sort of person who invited most callers inside, even Indians—at least into the yard, where there was shade. But in this case he felt that letting them through would admit their claim. He left them standing in the sun and sent out milk instead. As a courtesy, however, he ordered the dog back into the house.

Mr. Montovan was weighing several factors in his mind. As dishonest as he was with himself over his family life, he realized that he had married a woman too formidable to handle. He only admitted this to himself occasionally, and later pretended it wasn't the case at all. But it struck him with particular clarity that the accusation could make his youngest son more vulnerable to Miriam. His instinct was to protect Tommy and to figure out some way to treat the Indians equitably as well. He was a diplomat, given to solutions in which all parties were mildly satisfied and no one was overly concerned with justice. He was worried about Miriam's reaction, though, and came inside with a hard decisive expression he hoped his wife would find impenetrable.

"Well?" she asked.

"*Well*," he replied, "I'm going to talk to my son and find out what really happened here. That's what I'm going to do." He glared at her momentarily, but Miriam was unmoved and continued observing him with flickering distrust. He went downstairs.

Chaco did not have to wait long for his milk. The front door opened again, although more awkwardly this time, as Rafael was pulling the knob with one hand and holding both glasses with the other. He made a brief, unsuccessful effort to block the dog's exit with one of his legs, but decided it was a suicidal gesture and let the door swing open. The German shepherd bounded out and charged at the gate. The boy was so startled by the dog's ferocity that he jumped back, but his father only quivered slightly and remained still. Only now did Chaco observe that there was something very painful about the call to his father: his eyes were bitter and melancholy.

Rafael approached on the walkway holding a glass in each hand. He seemed to be moved by some distant regret, and did not regard the Indians too closely. He said "Good morning" in a way that was correct, but did not bother to speak above the din of the dog's barks. He handed Achuale and the boy their milk through the bars of the gate, taking care that the dog's lunges didn't cause any to spill. The German shepherd considered the cook a neutral obstacle; he knew not to bite him, but recognized him as a human without any real authority.

"Ar-Ar-Ar-Ar-Ar-Ar-Ar-Ar-Ar!"

Chaco held his glass with both hands and tried to relish the milk but was too frightened of the dog to get any real pleasure from it. He wondered at the distant and grave face of the cook, and looked into the glass as the marvelous white liquid emptied into his mouth. It tasted so good! And yet the harassment by the German shepherd, the heat, and the wait, were awful. When he was finished with the glass he handed it back shyly and said, "Gracias."

"Ah!" The cook favored him with a smile. But with Achuale the cook displayed his graver self. The two Indians nodded at each other as Achuale returned his glass, acting out a pantomime of mutual regret and embarrassment. Then Rafael walked into the house carrying both glasses, leaving Chaco to wonder what was happening with the gringo boy inside.

Mr. Montovan leaned into the doorway before entering Tommy's room. The boy pretended not to notice him at first, staring fixedly at an open book, but there was an unusual stiffness in his neck that betrayed self-consciousness. He was so glad his father came down instead of Miriam! The boy turned his head casually and said, "Oh. Hi, Daddy."

"Hi, Tommy."

Mr. Montovan sat down, looking out of place, as if he had mistaken the edge of the bed for a seat in a conference room. "There's an Indian waiting outside with his son. Do you know why they came here?"

"No."

There was no indication of any discomfort on the boy's face, and Mr. Montovan was startled at how well his son had learned to lie. It represented a kind of maturity that the father had completely overlooked. He realized it was inevitable in any child, and yet being confronted with it by his youngest boy saddened him. "They say you threw a rock at the boy and cut his cheek. It was some months ago. Did you do that, Tommy? Did you?"

"No, Daddy. I wouldn't do anything like that. Never." Tommy's face, showing the smooth suppleness of youth, was a picture of innocence, and his blue eyes, full of open curiosity, couldn't have complemented the expression more. Something about the perfection of the lie gave it a sad beauty.

Mr. Montovan observed the boy with an earnest sympathy that the boy found confusing. His father had a habit of leaning forward slightly when he listened to someone: it implied, in a deferential way, that he understood. "I'm not saying you did it, Tommy. I'm just trying to find out what happened. Now that Indian boy outside said someone cut him with a rock, and I don't think he's lying."

"I didn't do it, Daddy!"

"Do you know who did it?"

The boy paused. "No. I don't know anything about it." He spoke with a practiced sincerity. Even his heart, which had been beating wildly when his father came in, settled down to a regular pace. The lie had momentum now and required less effort to carry.

They could hear Miriam pacing upstairs. Though neither of them made any mention of her, the sound of her footsteps lent a sudden clarity to the situation. The impatient clicks continued briefly and went still.

"So you didn't do it, Tommy? You don't know anything about it?" Mr. Montovan's warm brown eyes said, "I understand."

"No, Daddy. I didn't do it. I wouldn't do anything to hurt a boy like that."

Though Mr. Montovan didn't believe Tommy, he chose to believe him. The lie settled in his mind and was accommodated there. "Well. That takes care of that, doesn't it?" he said with a decisiveness the boy admired. He got up and went upstairs.

"Well?" asked Miriam.

"He says he didn't do it."

"Oh!"

"When *my* son says he didn't do something, he didn't do it.

Who are you going to believe? The Indians out there?"

"Well *you're* his father. You *know*."

Mr. Montovan gave her an exasperated look and went out the door. He carried the lie with him into the sunlight. He felt a twinge of regret when he saw the Indians standing in place on the other side of the gate, and called off the dog immediately, cursing vaguely at whoever had been careless enough to let him out.

"My boy says he didn't do it," explained Mr. Montovan in the smooth, practiced way he had of addressing strangers. He was struck again by the formal presence of Señor Achuale; it made him uneasy.

There was a moment of silence. A lie is an awkward thing to catch, once it is spotted; and Achuale was considering a tactful way to deflect it. His son, who lacked the necessary subtlety to deal with the situation properly, piped in before his father had a chance to respond.

"He lied!" There was an awful wonder in Chaco's voice: his shock overwhelmed his indignation.

"He says he didn't do it," replied Mr. Montovan calmly. He looked at Chaco kindly and put his hands in his pockets. There was no hint in his manner of any contradiction between the Indians' claim and his son's response. "Perhaps," he said charitably, "there has been a misunderstanding. Perhaps I can help you out in some way. I would be glad to help you out in any way I can. The doctor—how much would it cost to treat this properly?"

Chaco found it hard to understand the American. On the one hand he seemed to deny any responsibility for the wound; on the other he seemed happy to fulfill any obligations incurred by his son's guilt. Despite the American's sympathy there was something missing from the situation. It was missing the idea of justice. To Chaco's mind the only satisfactory conclusion to the visit was for the gringo boy to admit what he'd done and accept the consequences for it. Instead the American was offering money and kindness, in such a way that the original purpose of the visit was obscured. The boy didn't know how to deal with it, and he looked to his father with his mouth open as Achuale weighed the moment's demands.

"If you believe your son has done nothing," said the Indian carefully, "then you owe us nothing."

"Well. Maybe I can help out in some way."

"Thank you, sir," said Achuale evenly. "But we can't take money from someone who owes us nothing. Certainly not from someone who does not believe what we say."

The insult was subtle but pointed, and Mr. Montovan looked down uncomfortably. He did not seem angry. "I only meant to help," he said in an offhand way that yet had an element of pleading to it.

Once more, in a polite and ritual manner, Achuale declined, and Chaco realized the claim had come to nothing. He saw clearly that his father's response was the only honorable one possible, that it was even laced with revenge. Yet a large part of him regretted that a middle way had not been accepted: one that was less respectable and possibly quite lucrative. Already he could sense his opening to the rich world closing, and with it the softness and luxury he associated with the glass of milk. The harder, more closely defined world of his own life was rearing up.

"So. There has been a misunderstanding," observed another voice from the front door.

"Miriam."

"Perhaps your son does not remember properly. Perhaps he needs to be reminded by looking the boy in the face, no? I think it might help him to remember."

"Miriam. Stay out of this. Now."

"I only mean to help," she replied playfully. "I will go get him."

"Miriam."

She looked back coyly, apparently encouraged by her husband's frustration. She went inside.

"Damn. Shitty bitch. Damn shitty bitch. Wait a moment,

please," added Mr. Montovan to the Indians in Spanish.

The German shepherd took advantage of his master's distraction to lunge at the Indians once more. This time Mr. Montovan arrested him at the collar and with unaccustomed brutality threw the dog back against the concrete walk. The dog yelped with shock at his master's betrayal and shied away with his head cocked to one side and his ears down.

Even Achuale showed surprise at the turn of events. He lowered his hat from its rigid position in front of his chest. Chaco felt a strange foreboding about what would happen next, and yet it seemed that the element of justice was re-entering the picture by a back way.

Miriam appeared at Tommy's door. "I thought you were here," she said, with the usual lazy edge to her voice. "You're wanted outside. You know what it's about."

"No," said Tommy helplessly.

"No, what? No you're not coming, or no you don't know?"

"I don't know."

"Huh!" she said indignantly. Then she relaxed a little. A lie was not such an affront to her authority as disobeying an order. "You don't know. How interesting. What a short memory you have. I thought your father just discussed this with you."

"Yes."

"Oh. 'Yes,' now. Yes. So you know what we're talking about."

"Uh-huh."

"Uh-*huh*. Well maybe you can put down the book you find so interesting and come upstairs with me. Do you think you can do that, Tommy?"

"Yes, Miriam."

"Uh-*huh*. And maybe you can look that Indian boy in the eye and *then* say you did nothing to hurt him. Can you do that?"

"Yes, Miriam."

"And maybe you can tell the truth. Do you know what happens to children who don't tell the truth?"

"Yes."

"They meet my belt. But you're so innocent, aren't you?"

"Uh-huh."

"I want you to say yes."

"Yes, Miriam."

"Come with me." She took his hand within the warm fingers of her own: her grip had the authority of a steel clasp, and her long painted nails ate into his skin—the sight of them had always made him think of how easily they could cut. She did not exactly pull him along; Tommy felt compelled to keep up with her, and together they marched up the stairs. When they passed the seashells Tommy felt nostalgia for the undersea world, but that comfort was fleeting. Rafael was wiping a dish in the kitchen, and observed the boy with a concerned, noncommittal expression. They went outside.

The scene looked like the aftermath of something. The dog had an injured look and was only half sitting up, as if afraid to commit himself to any one position. Tommy's father had his hands in his pockets and observed the approach of his wife and son warily. The Indians stood stiffly on the other side of the gate. The walkway was a gauntlet to Tommy. What was the right thing to do? No: he knew the right thing to do; what concerned him was how to survive the situation. He was surprised by the lack of anger in the shepherd boy's face, and if anything, the Indian boy's wonder made the moment more difficult for him. He fixed his attention on the scar: it struck him as a horrible miracle that his own mistake had left such a mark.

"Do you recognize him, Tommy?" asked Miriam in her insinuating way.

"No."

"*No*? Do you know what happens to children who lie?" She tugged his hand.

"Yes." Of course he knew—but he had already lied! What could he do? If he told the truth now he would be punished for lying *and* for hitting the boy. The possibilities were just too terrible, and as he watched the questioning face of the shepherd boy he felt the power of the lie pushing him on like a machine. It created a reality of its own, a fear greater than the shame he felt looking at the Indian's face. He was going to continue to lie, knowing full well God was going to punish him and that his soul was transparent even as he opened his mouth.

"I've never seen that boy before," he stated calmly.

"Oh! Did you hear that, Peter?"

"Well he *told* me that before, Miriam," said Mr. Montovan self-righteously.

"It's a lie!" said Chaco. He looked to his father. "He's lying, Papi!"

"Let's go."

"No. Wait," commanded Miriam. She looked at the Indians as if she had a surprise in store for them. "Wait. Tommy: are you telling me you've never seen this boy before?"

"Yes, Miriam."

"She looked at the Indians furtively, as if to say, *We know*, and then put her full attention on Tommy. "You've never seen him. You never threw a rock at him?"

"No."

Her face hardened into the sculpted features of a doll. With the change her eyes narrowed, becoming impenetrable. "I see a black streak running down your forehead. Crawling down little by little. I see a black *streak*."

Tommy was amazed that his stepmother was able to see such streaks when he had never caught them in a mirror. He wondered if it looked like a bruise; he also didn't quite believe her.

"I've never seen him before. I wouldn't do anything like that to hurt somebody."

Achuale put his hat back on. Chaco couldn't explain why, but he knew now there was no justice in the picture at all: they had been asked to stay for a different reason. He was beginning to feel like a spectator at something he wasn't supposed to witness. He was beginning to feel like—a servant.

"Let's go," repeated Achuale finally.

"Who are you doing this for, Miriam?" asked her husband sadly.

"He's not telling the truth!" She glared at her husband vehemently, but the effect she was after couldn't be realized. The Indians, with neither ceremony nor gesture, turned around and began walking downhill. They had simply given up, and so were beyond her, or anyone else's, control. Miriam let go of Tommy's hand, and he realized he had won a sort of victory over her. But his elation was mingled with a powerful sense of shame, and he worried about Jesus and his mother. He also knew that winning against Miriam meant that she would have certain revenge later—he didn't care to think what it would be. The boy excused himself meekly and went inside.

"There—are you going to let him get away?"

"Shit. He didn't do anything."

"Oh?" asked Miriam archly. "Oh?"

"Aw, hell—what do you think? Do all my children lie? Huh? Do they lie all the time? Is that what they do?"

"When they can get away with it."

"Aw, shit. You know what I think? I think you'd enjoy chewing garlic with that bitch in the kitchen. That's what I think."

Miriam actually seemed pleased by the insult. His offensive was made, now he would retreat. "Oh?" she asked calmly. "What exactly are you saying, Peter? That you don't like the way I'm raising the children? Are you saying that?"

"No, no, no," he replied irritably.

"I was just wondering," she said with a note of triumph. "You seemed to be implying that." She looked at him carefully and seemingly made her peace. She walked through the open door, and on a hunch, went over to the window in the dining room. It was as she thought: Tommy had made his escape to the back yard, and under the cool gaze of her eyes, was entering the world of Elfland at the bottom of the slope.

Mr. Montovan made up with his dog, thinking guiltily that nothing had been resolved fairly at all. There was nothing he could do for the Indians now—nothing.

By this time the Indians were a couple of blocks downhill. Chaco had gone along silently at first, but the injustice of the whole thing fired his mind so much that he couldn't hold out. "He lied!" he complained bitterly to his father. "He lied, he lied, he lied. And—and—and his father did nothing. And they let the dog bark at us! And—"

Achuale had been considering the same thing from a worldlier point of view. Very little of it surprised him; if anything his cynicism only acquired a keener edge. He already knew his son was a victim and there was nothing he could do about it. His only worry now was that Chaco would be hurt more and softened up by too much speculation on the matter. So he promptly replied "Shut up!" and the two of them made their way down on the undeveloped side of Bolivar, dodging cow-pies along the way.

Chapter Six

The lie had a powerful and lingering effect. When Chaco passed the Montovans' house in the mornings and afternoons, it always occurred to him that the gringo boy had thrown the rock at him and gotten away with lying about it. And as he recalled the unsuccessful visit he paid to the house with his father, he couldn't help thinking that the character of the place was based on a lie as well. It was the first time he had ever considered that the wealth of the neighborhood was based on something other than a degree of fortune much greater than his own.

His mother often said that the rich have a hard time getting into Heaven, but he had always assumed, with a child's intuition, that the saying was really an expression of envy. The neighborhood below the construction sites represented a life removed from his own, never attainable and yet strictly desirable. It was an exalted life God granted to only a few. Not knowing how the rich behaved, he could only observe the style of their luxury, and it was an example to him of the best way for a family to live. Now, however, as he went by with his sheep and looked at the yards and houses within the immaculate walls of the developed part of the slope, he detected the stir of corruption. Corruption within the beautiful houses and the exciting gardens all maintained by the unending labor of the servants: it was an idea new to the boy. He could think of nothing else but that the wealth and luxury of the neighborhood was founded on cheating by the rich against Indians like himself. Finding the worm within the idea of paradise made the neighborhood shabbier to him.

The boy found it strange to walk through a place where sin was hidden so subtly. Whereas he felt insignificant in the days before the incident, his heart was touched now with a spring of superiority. At times he even considered the architecture of the neighborhood a direct affront to the Lord—because it contained a lie. But it took concentration to remain so indignant, and most of the time he fell back to admiring the houses, wondering sadly why the people within them were not as good as he wanted them to be: especially the blond gods from the North.

Chaco's rubber boots were in worse shape than ever, and seemed to be worn as a purely formal gesture: they were so full of tears they couldn't protect his feet from much of anything. Though the red poncho and floppy hat looked ludicrous on his small body, the hardness in his face and posture, affectations of maturity, were more pathetic than laughable. He still treated the sheep horribly, with the "Hui!" and "Hoo!" particular to Indian shepherds. His round cheeks had kept their softness, however, and when he touched his scar, as he often did, it was with a look of bafflement, as if he had woken up with it, and wasn't sure what its presence on his face meant.

Every so often Chaco caught a glimpse of the blond boy in the yard as he headed downhill in the afternoon. The first time the gringo pretended not to see him, and Chaco studied the figure of his enemy with seething resentment. A couple of days later the gringo did look back, however, and once again they stared at each other from opposite sides of the road. It made Chaco very uncomfortable. Not only did he feel humiliated by the gringo's invulnerability, but also the blond watched him with a questioning look that was hard to understand. What did it mean? It brought back the question of the boy's original motive. Chaco even wondered if the boy felt bad about what he'd done, and oddly enough, felt a moment of sympathy for him. The slight softening of his attitude made the memory of the incident more painful, and he couldn't help trying to share his confusion with his father.

"I saw the gringo boy again today, Papi," he said, once the sheep were in the pen. "He looked back at me."

"And what?" returned Achuale brusquely. "Does that change anything?"

What could the boy say to that? That the machinery of doubt made things difficult to judge and even harder to express? Or that he felt lonely in a way that no one could understand?

It never occurred to Chaco that the one person who might have understood his feelings was the gringo boy. Yet it was Tommy who wondered the most about the shepherd's life. When his stepmother punished him for some infraction, he thought that he deserved to be hurt after all—because of what he had done to the shepherd boy. And when he considered that his life wasn't nearly as pleasant as when his mother was alive, he realized it was only natural—because of what he had done to the shepherd boy. He accepted the retribution and began relating it to the central question of his life. Why did his mother die and leave them behind on earth?

He had always considered his mother's death accidental and unfair. But now he speculated that there was a design behind her loss. Perhaps Jesus was aware of the imperfections in his character, and those of the other children: and left them with Miriam to scour away their flaws. Tommy had so much faith in God that he assumed there was an element of mercy in anything that happened, and he resolved that the cramped unhappiness of Miriam's household was necessary to becoming the person he was meant to be.

It made him look at Miriam in a new way. Not with love, certainly, but he developed a respect for her that did not have to do entirely with fear. She was an instrument of God's will. She may not be aware of the fact, but an instrument she was, and this gave coherence to her moods. When she went on a rampage, he reminded himself that the finger of God was behind it, and the moment became easier to bear. He even began to wonder if he shouldn't feel some affection for her, and when he quivered at the sound of her footsteps upstairs or her voice down the hall, he reminded himself, "I should love her, she is doing the best thing for me."

His private thoughts weren't known to anyone. Outwardly Tommy was the same, and the earnest expression in his blue eyes hadn't changed. He still wore the bright, striped shirts that made him look like a pet, and he spent a lot of time in the yard. Only Miriam was aware that he was more complacent. While he had never been openly rebellious, she had often noticed a burning resentment in his eyes when she administered punishment. Now he accepted everything and simply repeated, "Yes, Miriam." But the change didn't satisfy her because she didn't understand it and couldn't control it.

Even Rafael noticed how Miriam began observing the boy more closely. She was aware of how quickly he retreated to his room after school, and how he went immediately to the flowerbeds once his homework was done. She walked from the kitchen to the dining room when she heard the outer door open downstairs, and gazed out the window as the boy approached the slope in the backyard. She realized he didn't leave the property as much as before, and began questioning the cook and Mariella about how the boy spent his time. Occasionally Rafael heard his wife grunt with a "Huh!" when the Señora went to spy on the boy: she might as well have said, "His time is up." One afternoon the cook glanced out of the slit-shaped window in the kitchen, and saw the Señora gazing at the shepherd boy as he came down the mountain shouting "Hui!" at the sheep and waving his staff. His mongrel was trotting along the fringes of the flock, driving the German shepherd at the Señora's side crazy. Rafael remembered the morning the Indians came to make their case, and his observation of the scene made him uneasy. But he said nothing about it to his wife, and it wasn't apparent the Señora's spying was leading to any particular conclusion.

After the lie proved so successful, Tommy felt compelled to spend time in the front yard once or twice a week. His encounters with the shepherd boy made him profoundly uneasy, however, and he preferred the more secure environment of Elfland in the back, where he hid most afternoons. Yet whenever Segundo had a new plant to show him by the front wall, he showed enthusiasm and followed him there, always flattered by the Indian's enigmatic friendship. On several occasions he was playing in the front when the shepherd boy came down with his flock, and Tommy felt a burning sensation in the back of his neck until the group passed by. Whenever he could he pretended not to notice them. The times when he looked up inadvertently and they faced each other, Tommy was struck by the reality of what he'd done. It didn't seem possible that the scar on the shepherd's cheek was his own doing; yet it was. He watched the boy with apprehension, always wondering what the expression in the Indian's eyes meant, and if the boy could ever forgive him. Their relationship amounted to a pantomime of misunderstood looks. When Tommy saw the shepherd he noticed how Chaco paused each time he passed the house, gazing at the fountains and the trees, as if remembering where his injury came from.

Tommy never went back to the plateau. In his mind the place was dreadful; for in spite of its beauty, the grassy field was where the worst part of his character had revealed itself. He even avoided the construction sites, and from the front yard observed the changing character of the houses on the twisting road above him. At a glacial pace, and depending on how much money was coming in from the owners, the different lots were assuming the appearance architects had planned for them. Clusters of steel rods became concrete columns, cement block formed walls where spaces had been; new walls were painted. Fairly soon it would cease to be a place of afternoon adventures and become just another part of the neighborhood. Occasionally Tommy wondered what the guards would do when the area was finished. He imagined that eventually the neighborhood would encroach on the plateau as well, probably long after he had left the country. The meadow, with its boulders and cattle under the close sky, would become real estate, and the boy wondered where the Indian shepherds would go when the last of the common grazing areas on the mountain was taken away. What would it mean when the characteristics of a place that meant so much to him were simply erased from the earth? The idea of it made him sad, and it seemed a crime that the place, and his sin, and the Indians would be forgotten.

After a while it took an effort for him to feel as guilty about the situation as before. A month after the lie, Tommy often reminded himself that he was not as good a person as he seemed to others; but there was something vaguely mechanical in his repetition of the thought. He knew well enough that his mother and Jesus were in on everything and saw the worst part of his nature, but he tended to accept the merciful aspect of their love, and felt more grateful to them than shamed.

One afternoon began much like the others. The school bus dropped him off in the middle-class neighborhood at the bottom of the mountain, and he and Geoffrey spent a moment gazing into the window of a tienda that had a generous display of pastries. Then they began walking uphill. In the distance a church bell was ringing the hours, a bright signal that there was freedom until dinner. It was three o'clock. The boys walked with giddy energy, and an expectant look about them, and Tommy thought longingly of Mrs. O'Donnell's tapioca. But when his friend's mother came to the gate she only said, "How are the days keeping you, Tommy?" and gave him a wry smile. He understood that there would be no pudding that afternoon, and continued uphill with considerably less enthusiasm.

But he still felt happiness that could only be explained in terms of his light-headed freedom. With the oppression of his guilt nearly worn away, he took pleasure in observing the undeveloped slope on the right side of the road, eyeing the new construction sites further up, and imagining the wars he could set in them with his friends. When he got to his own house a feeling of constriction came over him again, but lifted after Rafael buzzed open the gate.

He heard Miriam's voice in the kitchen, decided it was not safe to ignore it, and yelled out a gay-sounding "Hello!" to her. Then he quickly went downstairs.

There was definitely only one thing to do on an afternoon like this, when he had no homework, and felt so free: go outside. So he gave perfunctory greetings to Billy, who had gotten to the room first, and to his sister, left his book bag on the bed, and picked up a toy. As he passed the staircase in the servants' quarters he noticed a strong smell from the litter boxes and overheard Miriam talking to the cook. It had something to do with dinner, but there was a gossipy kind of banter with it that was her version of the common touch.

Tommy made directly for the slope in the back and felt euphoric as he entered the radiant corner of Elfland. It was at the bottom of the yard, where a low stone wall marked the edge of the property, and the tree that grew there was at the heart of his imagination. Cool moss lapped over its roots, and plenty of flowers grew like guardians among them. A hummingbird suspended itself nearby as it sucked on an orange alstromelias. Arriving at that section of the yard played a trick on his mind, and the present dropped away. The earlier part of his life came near, and as he entered a reverie of nostalgia and fantasy Jesus and his mother seemed closer than ever. Segundo, sensitive to the boy's moods, never disturbed him there. That's why it was unusual to hear footsteps approaching an hour after he arrived.

His first assumption was that the gardener had some business at the bottom of the hill. But there was lightness in the tread as well as a kind of lazy authority; and Tommy knew whom the steps belonged to. Miriam's approach to this part of the yard was unprecedented and frightened him. He felt his back stiffen as the steps crunched on the grass, and the prosaic reality of his little corner reasserted itself. The chattering of elves in the boughs was actually air rustling in the leaves; the moss at the roots of the tree was not a sea. The only thing approaching an elf was the toy he called Noddy, who was quite dirty and sat limply against the tree's bark. The footsteps came to a stop almost directly behind him, and in the silence that ensued he could hear the beating of his own heart.

"Hello, Tommy."

"Hi Miriam," said the boy with an affected chirpiness. There was an undercurrent of fear in his voice. He turned his head to glance at her, and was particularly mindful of her white sandals and the pinpoint dots on her legs from being shaved in the morning. Somehow his awareness of the labor that went into her appearance, and the slightly imperfect results that came out of it, made her even more oppressive.

"I've noticed that you have a little friend," said Miriam.

For a moment Tommy thought she was referring to the elf-doll, and he was caught completely off-guard. The line of attack—if that's what it was—was so indirect he wasn't sure how to respond. His fantasy world was so private he would feel defenseless if he admitted her into it just a little. So he picked up the doll in an off-hand way and dropped it back rather roughly, as if it meant nothing to him. Miriam watched the action without any particular interest, but seemed to take note of it, as she did all details that might have relevance later.

"I've been noticing him for some time now," she continued patiently. "He stops in front of the house every afternoon on his way downhill. Then he looks in—looking for you, his little friend. It's become a regular habit of his. Very touching. Do you know who I'm talking about, Tommy?"

"No."

"No?" she repeated with an air of disapproval, yet as if she took some pleasure in his response.

"Uh-uh."

"Look at me."

The boy turned, straining his neck. The sun had fallen to the other side of the city and was almost directly behind his stepmother's head. Her hair burned radiantly, and for all appearances, he might have been squinting out of fear and awe of her, and not because of the afternoon glare.

"I think you might remember him if you saw him again. I think so." She dropped the words with pitiless irony. "Do you remember the cholo boy who came here with his father not so long ago?"

"Uh-huh."

"Uh-*huh*. Have you forgotten how to say yes or no?"

"Yes, I remember him."

"Yes." She paused, relishing the flavor of the word, observing the boy with a coolness touched by gaiety. "You don't play in the front yard much, do you, Tommy?"

"Sometimes I do."

"Oh? Sometimes?" She laughed in a way that was almost friendly; and again Tommy thought her manner indecipherable. "But not very much this time of the afternoon, I suppose. Not very much. Otherwise you would see your little friend, wouldn't you?"

The boy felt too helpless to say anything, and squinted at her once more, meeting the direct gaze of her copper eyes. They expressed a penetrating, comprehensive intelligence that seemed to understand everything about him, and pervade everything. There was a softness in her look that belonged to a person of great empathy and compassion; but the empathy and compassion were not there. The boy found it hard to understand what kind of mind he was dealing with; he only understood what was missing from it.

"You're very innocent, aren't you, Tommy? Your father swears by it. You look so innocent. I've been very impressed by how innocent you look. You're much better at it than your brothers and sister. I must say you threw me off for a while. Are you innocent, Tommy?"

"Uh-huh," replied the boy, with the helpless slow awareness that he was being led somewhere.

"Uh-huh," repeated Miriam, without her usual emphasis on the second syllable. "And what are you innocent of, may I ask?"

"Nothing," said the boy timidly. He looked at the grass, sensing that he was in the trap already, and would be caught in his lie, or in some contradiction. But she seemed bored by the pursuit and simply studied him for a while with her arms crossed. Tommy squinted at her once more.

"Will you do me a favor?" she asked.

"Yes, Miriam."

"Yes, this time," she noted archly. "I would like you to come with me. Will you do that? Come with me."

She extended a white arm rather languidly, and Tommy stood up with reluctance and took her hand. He hesitated, wondering whether to bring the elf or not; then left it sitting on the tree's roots. Miriam glanced at the boy with a mixture of curiosity and detachment, then led the way uphill. Her grip had a kind of softness to it, though there was firmness beneath that gave no hint of sympathy. Her skin was moist and pleasant to the touch, yet Tommy felt he was betraying something by holding her hand. She pulled at his arm just enough to remind him that he had no choice in coming to their destination; yet her face was more bored than angry. With no particular hurry they walked up the steep grass to the flat section of the back, and passed Segundo, who tactfully pretended not to notice what was going on. Tommy felt abandoned by everybody, and that it was nobody's fault: he knew that he deserved what was coming. Justice lay above the stone steps where Miriam led him, and up they went, he always one step behind. At the top step a lazy gray Persian was sunning herself and didn't bother to get out of Miriam's way. The boy stepped over the cat with some respect.

Once they were in the front yard Miriam looked over to the path the Indians took to the plateau. Apparently satisfied that they had arrived early enough, she pulled Tommy over to the deck. She had him sit down on the edge of it, and after surveying the area of the constructions sites above the house she lit a cigarette and sat beside him. There was something impersonal in her manner: she seemed distantly angry at the boy, not so much for what he had done, as that he had done it beyond her control. And oddly enough, as he sat next to her, Tommy sensed that he had no real history with the woman, or relationship; what held them together was a kind of law, and the law was entirely in her hands. The world of natural feelings seemed irrelevant as he waited on Miriam's fine sense of justice. They both regarded the intersection of the path with the Avenida Bolivar, but Tommy regarded it far more reluctantly.

"I think he will see us here, will he not, as he comes downhill with the sheep?" asked Miriam, after she exhaled a drag of smoke. She didn't seem to expect a reply, and glancing at the boy, crossed her legs and waited.

She was definitely an attractive woman. As Tommy looked at her ever so timidly, he marveled again at the work that went into her appearance. There was such a fine sense of tact and judgment in the way her face was made up, and her nails painted, that he could only respect her for the intelligence it showed, and certainly for its effect. But the element of calculation and vanity in her looks frightened him.

In the late afternoon sunlight her hair had a luxuriant radiance that made it seem infinitely pliable to the touch; but as he looked more closely there was something stiff about the styling, and the texture of the strands was wrong. He concluded she was wearing one of her wigs. In this way Tommy sat there, torn between an attraction for his stepmother and fear and repulsion of her. His indecisiveness made him even more helpless than perhaps Miriam ever intended, as he was caught between his need to love and be loved, and his inability to understand the woman who had so much power over him. He bided his time by poking the grass gently with his feet, and called for the dog when he came trotting up the steps. The German shepherd responded immediately, but to Tommy's dismay he showed no preference for the boy over his stepmother, and accepted her attentions just as eagerly.

After awhile Miriam leaned forward slightly as she smoked. She had an air of poise that implied she was a woman of substance at ease in the luxury of her surroundings. She wasn't spoiled into dullness, however, for there was attentiveness in her manner that communicated a great and aesthetic pleasure in the fountains behind her, the colors of Segundo's garden, the air, and the pets in the yard. The boy was her charge; everything about the place was as it was meant to be, and everything was meant for her. Her appearance suspended the belief that anything outside her attention really mattered. She was fascinating to watch. Occasionally a rare look of sadness came over her, suggesting a depth and caring in her nature that made her even more intriguing. But her only comment to the boy all this time was to observe, after looking down at him in a flinty and careless way, that, "If you keep on kicking the grass with your sneakers, you know they're going to turn green."

As the sun dipped over the range of mountains behind them, dragging away the color in the neighborhood, gray tones lingered over the construction sites. A sheep appeared at the head of the path and then another, their coats almost camouflaged against the twilight. They were limping, still unused to their freedom from the ropes and unenthusiastic about the pen awaiting them downhill. Then the mongrel appeared, running to keep the sheep in check and the only animal among the flock taking pleasure in his duty. It seemed the longest interval before the shepherd himself turned the corner behind the flock, issuing his cruel "Hui's!" and brandishing his staff.

His heart quickening, Tommy waited for the Indian boy to notice them. Miriam looked satisfied as she sighed, "Ah. Your little Indian friend. Here he comes." She exhaled a cool puff of smoke.

But Chaco did not see them right away or even bother to look up. He was musing on an occurrence that afternoon that bothered him. A group of Indian kids—how old were they? teenagers?—had walked across the plateau in sight of him. They seemed to have nothing in particular to do and nowhere in particular to go. That by itself was not much. But he also heard them murmur, "Shepherd boy. Ha! Ha! Ha!" Their tone made it clear they did not feel friendly toward him, and he remembered noticing them a couple of times before, passing across the plateau. They had watched him, much as the blond gods had watched him carefully from a distance before making their attack. He was not sure whether to mention the incident to his father.

As Chaco got close to the intersection of the path and the Avenida Bolivar he looked up out of habit, as Miriam expected him to. Was it habit as well that made him touch his cheek as he saw the woman and the boy sitting in front of the fountains? Chaco came to a stop.

"There he is. He recognizes you. His little friend," said Miriam airily. "Shall we greet him, Tommy? I'm sure he would appreciate that. Let us greet him." She stood up, stamping the cigarette into the grass (Segundo would clean it up), and put out her hand.

The German shepherd, alerted to the presence of the mongrel across the street, began trotting back and forth along the fence with raspy "Arf's!" as a prelude to his real barking fit.

Chaco was surprised that the two gringos looked back at him. Usually the blond boy pretended not to notice him, but now the two foreigners stared back so intently he suspected they had actually been waiting for him. Why? Then they stood up and approached the fence walking hand in hand. The mother had an imperious air and seemed to have an object in mind; the boy accompanied her meekly. The woman stopped ten feet short of the fence and directed a question to her charge. A glance at Chaco informed the Indian that she counted his presence; but the lassitude in her face implied that she did not count it for very much. The German shepherd, taking their approach as a cue, snarled viciously, kicking up dirt as he ran along the posts.

"He recognizes you, doesn't he, Tommy?" asked Miriam with a sugary voice. "He recognizes you so well. His little friend. Why does he recognize you so well?"

The boy said nothing, pursing his lips with the utmost concentration. He felt his conscience being rummaged by Jesus himself, and looked at the Indian boy, almost imploring him for help. Miriam squeezed his hand with steely fingers.

"It's very touching how he looks back at you. Is he remembering something, perhaps? Is he remembering a little prank, maybe? Did one of us throw a rock at him once—maybe? Or are we very innocent here? Well, Tommy?"

"I don't know, Miriam. I don't know him."

"Look him in the face. Come on now, Tommy."

"I don't know him. I would never do anything to hurt somebody like that."

Chaco stared at the two of them wonderingly.

"Really?" asked Miriam with an edge to her voice. "Really?" She didn't seem bothered by the ruckus the dog was making; the chaos may well have been an intended effect. It made the shepherd boy, enduring the vicious barks, all the more pathetic.

The mongrel dog, while not returning the fury of the German shepherd, seemed sorely tempted. Occasionally while running back and forth along the line of sheep he stopped and returned a bark before remembering his other duty. The sheep began getting confused. Not being urged from behind or kept in check by the dog, a couple of them wandered into the street until redirected by the horn of a car passing uphill.

"I don't know him," repeated Tommy.

Miriam's grip became tighter as she drew up his hand and said: "Look at me."

The boy looked into the copper eyes that were so intelligent and so flat, and made a prayer to his mother. He could feel a black streak moving down his forehead like a slug; but Miriam, who searched his face, didn't claim to have discovered it herself.

"Where did you and that Irish boy play when you went uphill after school all those times?" she demanded.

Her intuition was so exact that Tommy couldn't help feeling a surge of respect for her. He replied, "Those houses. The ones they're building up there."

Miriam continued studying him without lowering his hand or relaxing her grip. She had the look of someone who has reduced a search to a very small area, and confident of claiming her object, postponed the inevitable catch. "We haven't greeted your friend, have we?" she observed whimsically. "I think we should. Let us greet him and acknowledge that you remember him as well. It would be nice, wouldn't it? Let us wave at him. Wave, Tommy." She squeezed his hand until it hurt.

Tommy raised his arm hesitantly. Miriam, observing the mechanical nature of his greeting, squeezed his hand tighter. "Wave," she said, with none of the artifice left in her voice. "Wave to your little friend."

Chaco watched the display incredulously. He once would have believed that the greetings were as friendly as they appeared to be, and he would have allowed his anger to melt away. But the experiences of the past two months had had their effect. He made no effort to wave back and realized the other boy was simply obeying his mother. Chaco took a malicious pleasure in seeing the little god so utterly dominated by someone else.

Then the woman herself waved. She waved with such airy casualness that the gesture seemed perfectly natural; and despite himself Chaco wanted the hardness in his heart to melt away so that he could return the greeting and be a friend. But she didn't wave just once or twice. She kept on waving, more slowly and mechanically, until her persistence seemed like a taunt. Then she stretched her arm to the utmost and her movements became as exaggerated as her smile. But Chaco simply stared back until the woman gave up getting a reaction out of him. She stopped abruptly and laughed.

"Ha ha ha ha ha ha!"

The harshness in the woman's laughter was out of keeping with her beauty, and it had a strangely impersonal quality. She did not seem to be laughing specifically at him, or even at the gringo boy; she might as well be laughing at herself. The laugh made light of everything. Not for the first time Chaco felt used by the woman for some inexplicable end. He felt a rush of humiliation and glared at her before calling to the dog and continuing downhill.

"Ha ha ha ha ha ha!"

Shortly afterwards Chaco looked back and saw that the blond boy had given up waving and looked defeated. It was no consolation to the Indian, however, and he hit a sheep that got out of line with a whack of real reproach.

Miriam continued holding Tommy's hand. As the shepherd got further away her grip softened and acquired a tenderness that was almost comforting. The look of irony on her face melted away, leaving her wistful as she watched the Indian carrying on with cries of "Hui!" and "Hoo!" Again Tommy sensed a depth and vulnerability which she rarely let show. He had an uncomfortable feeling of collaboration with her and didn't know what to make of her laugh.

Miriam didn't say anything. She held his hand naturally and seemed to have forgotten herself. Then she looked into Tommy's face searchingly. "What would your mother have thought of you?" she asked softly. She let his hand go and squeezed his shoulder reassuringly before turning away to the house. She walked slowly, with less determination than usual, her head to one side with a burden of thought. Tommy felt bound to her, if only by the secret they shared. As he watched her pretty figure recede, he couldn't help wondering if he was supposed to love her, and if she didn't deserve to be loved after all.

Chapter Seven

The memory of the American woman's laughter made Chaco melancholy as he approached his family's hut. The sound kept playing in his mind and the sight of his home brought little comfort. Her mockery made everything he did, and every aspect of his life, seem unimportant.

As usual he herded the sheep into the pen, and when he closed the gate to the enclosure he felt done with them. To Chaco the confusion of the animals and their perpetual stupidity was exasperating. He sat down on a rock stuck rigidly in the packed dirt around the enclosure and watched the violet depression of the evening. He even condescended to pet the dog and got pleasure out of it, for there was something infectious about the dog's enthusiasm. But the dog left him to chase a crow that had settled on the gate, and didn't seem to need him after that.

From the flickering glow inside the hut and the lack of voices he was aware that his mother had lit the fire for dinner and that his father hadn't come home. He went inside, sat on a stool by the door, and watched his mother stirring the beans over the fire. She looked up at him.

"Hello Chaquito. How did it go?"

"All right, Mama."

"Ah." The baby's whimpering distracted her. She adjusted the pouch on her back until he was silent and looked out from his confinement with perplexed concentration. Then his mother began humming, and Chaco leaned forward on his stool, resting his elbows on his knees, to listen.

His father came home later than usual. He offered no explanation and took a seat across the room without saying hello. He didn't ask for dinner, but simply waited to be served. Chaco's mother stopped humming. Sylvia was called in from a neighboring hut, the twins trudged up with water from the stream, and the beans were ladled into bowls with their complement of dry bread.

"How did it go today, eh, Chaco?" asked Achuale as he soaked the bread in his beans.

"Normal." Replied the boy.

"Normal." That was what his father wanted to hear. It didn't matter what really happened; it was enough to know that the boy was tough enough to bear it. Chaco didn't say anything more. He knew that his father studied him with much greater sympathy than the tone of his question implied. He even felt proud of himself.

But what was he to do about the other Indian boys? While he mulled over the beans on his lap (which were as bland as usual, and even less filling) he pictured them wandering over the plateau watching him with careless laughter. Were they drunk? Chaco had a special fear of drunks, for while none had ever bothered him, they represented in his mind the total disintegration of character. What did it mean if even children were drunk? Where were their parents?

"Oh! Someone poked me in the back!" shrieked Sylvia. "It was you!" She accused one or the other of the twins—both held their spoons aggressively.

"It was him Papi! It was him! I swear, swear, swear!"

"No, no, no! It was him!"

The twins betrayed each other casually, without a hint of anger. It made distinguishing between them even more difficult, and Achuale, who didn't have the patience to understand their relationship, observed the squabble indifferently. One was innocent, one was guilty. They were both innocent, they were both guilty. Finally Chaco leaned toward them and snapped, "Shut up, you little pigs!"

It silenced them. His sister looked at him gratefully, and the twins, observing him with sullen respect, went back to stirring their spoons in their beans. His mother looked unhappy, but in his father's face Chaco detected a subtle pride. Chaco felt pleased with himself until he wondered if it was his scar that had frightened the twins.

After dinner he kicked a can around in the semi-darkness with some of the neighboring kids, and recognized the deference with which they got out of his way when he tried to make a goal. Was it his new ugliness that made them wary? After the game he went back to the pen where the sheep huddled and leaned against a post, stroking his cheek, memorizing the details of the crevice there. He didn't notice his sister watching him until the mongrel ran up to her and poked her with his snout.

"Is something wrong, Chaquito?"

He said no, but she continued waiting. "I saw something on the plateau today," he admitted finally. "Some other Indian kids like us—just hanging around, watching me. Then they started laughing at me, chanting 'Shepherd Boy, Shepherd Boy'—like it was a joke!"

"They were drunk?" asked the girl.

"Yes."

"How awful!"

"Papi isn't supposed to know about this. I can handle it myself."

"He's not?" asked the girl in a hushed tone.

"Don't tell him anything. Then, later on, I came down into the rich neighborhood, and saw the gringo there, the one who cut me on the cheek. He was waiting for me with his mother. They waved at me."

"They waved?"

"And then they walked closer to the fence and his mother laughed at me. She laughed like a witch!"

"Those people!"

Chaco nodded uncomfortably; he wasn't satisfied by his own words. How could he tell his sister about the perversity he sensed, and the beauty of the house hiding such terrible people? He didn't understand any of it, and for the rest of the evening the boy was haunted by the distant taunts he heard on the plateau and the unnatural laughter of the woman in the brilliant, protected garden.

How was it possible to decipher Miriam? In the hours before dinner Tommy was mesmerized by the idea that she had something in store for him, and feared that she was going to humiliate him at the table. She often announced the discovery of a crime as the family was gathered around, and Tommy thought she might use the occasion to extract a confession. What a temptation it was to let everything out! But he knew he wouldn't, because he couldn't bear to let his family know how much meanness there was in his nature. Still, the odd way Miriam had squeezed his shoulder before going back into the house unsettled him more than any punishment he could think of.

He stayed outside until it was time for Segundo to go home. After he said goodbye to the gardener he watched him go downhill with the small bag that carried his lunch over his shoulder. He felt a sudden longing to go after him and find out what kind of house he lived in and what his family was like. For when Segundo went to his hut he left the world of Miriam completely behind, and Tommy had a feeling that a show of great complexity was being organized inside the house. He saw Miriam walking from one room to another on the main floor giving orders to the servants; and the servants were going into other rooms to obey them. He saw his sister lightly walk upstairs, and then his father with heavier steps. He knew that they too would be drawn into the plan, but that he himself was the real target.

Then he suddenly remembered: the elf doll was still at the foot of the dogwood tree! Tommy ran down the stone steps to the lower yard feeling virtuous and useful, certain that his mother would be proud of him for rescuing the toy. From what? Darkness? Uncertainty? The cool evening air? It didn't matter: he wasn't going to leave it abandoned in the yard. He found the elf sitting in the dark grass with his permanent cheery smile, picked him up, and felt relieved trudging up the slope to the back door.

As he passed the servants' stairway to the kitchen he heard Miriam saying, "What's that? What's that doing there?" The response, which he couldn't hear, was followed by her harsh, insinuating laughter. He entered the main downstairs hallway, and saw that Richard was in his room studying a meticulously assembled model of an F-4 Phantom, fantasizing about being a pilot. Richard didn't notice him, so he walked directly to the room he shared with Billy and sat down at the desk. Billy, who had been lying on his bed, looking bored, propped himself up on an elbow. He was darker than Tommy and born to mischief.

"Are you going to sit there and read *Time* magazine?" he asked sarcastically.

"No, I was going to read something else."

"I wish you wouldn't be such a dork all the time, reading *Time* magazine. It's embarrassing having a little brother who's always trying to prove he's a dork."

"I am not a dork."

Billy sat up fully on the bed and sighed. "You're a dork."

"How much time do you have left?" asked Tommy.

"Three more days stuck in here. I've counted all the steps from here to every other room I'm allowed to go to. It's twelve steps to the bathroom. It's seventy-five steps to the dining room. That's if you go up one stair at a time."

"How many steps from the front door?"

"I forgot."

Billy's crime, which was to hide tomatoes in his cheek until after dinner and then spit them out in the toilet (he was discovered by Miriam because he forgot to flush), led to a sentence of three weeks confined to his room after school. He also had to write, one thousand times over, "I will always eat my tomatoes." He spent his time under restriction as unproductively as possible, drawing pictures of naked girls that he showed to Tommy after bedtime with a flashlight.

Since at least one of the children was always being punished, there was little to distinguish this evening from any other. The only thing unusual was that Katy went upstairs before anyone else. It worried Tommy: why would she go to the kitchen when Miriam was already there?

Mr. Montovan, a dim voice upstairs, called everyone to dinner. The boys obeyed with grim anticipation. Richard walked up first, with Billy behind him. Tommy was the last to arrive because he carefully counted each step from his desk to his place at the table and came up with seventy-seven. Tommy and Billy stood behind their chairs on one side of the table while Mr. Montovan helped seat Miriam. Richard, as the eldest son, seated his sister. He performed the duty with a rigid face, and Katy was mildly pleased to see him so tortured. Rafael and his wife showed no reaction to the ritual as they busied themselves bringing out plates of food from the kitchen. Once Miriam was seated satisfactorily Mr. Montovan took his own chair, and on that signal the boys sat down.

Dinner always began with a glass of guava juice. Why guava juice, as opposed to some other variety, no one had the courage to ask anymore, and guava juice it was. The children drank it like medicine, and then Rafael brought out a pitcher of milk.

"Well!" said Mr. Montovan with feigned enthusiasm. "Now that we're all sitting here together, I was wondering whether anything interesting happened to any of you today. Do any of you children have anything to, uh—contribute?"

When they were alone, the children took great pleasure in imitating this one question of their father's, which always seemed to follow the guava juice and precede the milk. Its more immediate effect, however, was to encourage Tommy, Billy, and Katy to stare thoughtfully into their plates. Richard, who had never gotten over his father's submission to Miriam, looked at him with probing, defensive eyes.

"Well!" said Mr. Montovan with an unflappable but puzzled air.

The door to the kitchen swung open, and out came the cook with a tray supporting two large bowls. The door swung again, and out followed his wife with the rest of the offering. Whatever animosity the couple felt for each other, they behaved with perfect deference to their masters, and couldn't have served the meal more smoothly. At these times Mariella even managed to convert her usual sour expression into a subtle look of disappointment. They placed the serving dishes in the middle of the table, and then stood composed on either side. Though Rafael often winked at Tommy while serving dinner, he didn't do so tonight. He only looked to the head of the table with alert, quizzical eyes, and since Mr. and Mrs. Montovan did not respond, returned with his wife to the kitchen.

It was a pity, considering the effort that went into presenting the meal that its quality wasn't more consistent. The first bowl passed around the table contained a batch of salad left over from the day before. (There was no waste in this house, Miriam explained, not when there were Indians starving on the same hill.) It had been pickled overnight in yesterday's dressing, leaving the lettuce and tomatoes soggy with vinegar. A bowl of lima beans followed that wonderful dish. They were nobody's favorite either, but Miriam decreed that since the Indians ate them, the children should have regular helpings as well. Rafael had given up trying to make them interesting, preferring to devote his talents to the dishes Miriam didn't supervise. Tonight these were a sweet potato casserole and some steak. Tommy relished the smell of these last two dishes as he served them onto his plate, but was careful to eat the beans and salad first, and not too quickly or slowly. Miriam considered a regular eating pace a sign of etiquette.

Forks clicked against the plates, sometimes together, more often with random scrapes, and food went into everyone's mouths. The children didn't utter a word between bites and chewed self-consciously. This way the meal went on, well after the salad was eliminated, until an insistent click emerged within the irregular pattern of scrapes. It was the sound of a fork striking a plate, lightly and deliberately. Richard was piercing and eating his lima beans one by one, his form of protest almost unnoticeable until he began to murmur, "Um. Mm. Mmm!" with each bite.

"What?" asked Miriam sharply.

"Oh, I just lo-oove lima beans," he replied languorously.

"Good! You will have them tomorrow as well. As usual."

"Oh. Well, tha-ank you, Miriam."

She studied him carefully, but did not seem threatened by the display. Instead she went back to her food, smiling absently as if she were reminded of something. Her expression, as well as her refined movements cutting her steak, gave her an appearance of great delicacy. At moments such as this her poise came easily, her natural beauty seemingly animated by the subtle thoughts turning in her mind. She pretended not to notice that the children were alert to her every movement, obviously deriving pleasure from the effect of her nonchalance. She was in no hurry to reveal where her thoughts were leading, and took for granted that her audience would be ready whenever she spoke her mind. In the meantime dinner continued with the plodding sounds of forks and knives tapping and scraping the plates as the children worked through the lima beans toward Rafael's more eagerly awaited delicacies. Just as Tommy reached the steak a particularly pleasing thought seemed to move Miriam, for the faintest blush came over her cheeks. She put down her knife and fork and mused, "I saw something interesting today." To all appearances, she was responding to the question with which Mr. Montovan had begun the meal.

"Oh—really?" asked her husband owlishly.

"Yes. I spent some time in the garden." She glanced at Tommy with a brusque expression of warning. Tommy's body stiffened as he anticipated his humiliation.

"I went to the garden," she repeated thoughtfully as she looked away from Tommy's face. "I took the back door to get there, and as I passed Katy's room I noticed that her door was closed." Miriam paused just long enough for the information to have an effect, but Katy, who suddenly realized she was the target, held her fear in check with great restraint. Tommy wondered why Miriam was going on a tangent.

"I thought nothing of it. I thought: Maybe she's changing. (Though why a girl her age would want to change twice a day is beyond me.) I passed by her door and went outside. I was out in the garden for quite a long time." She glanced again at Tommy. "When I came back inside, some time later, the door was still closed. It had been closed for over an hour now. And I thought, well—maybe she did change. Maybe she just forgot to open her door again. But an hour. So I called her upstairs. And when she came upstairs I saw that she had not changed. So the question remains, why was her door closed for an hour, and what was she doing in there all that time?"

The confusion that came over Katy's face was terrible to watch. She did not understand the nature of the attack, and knew that no one was going to defend her. She looked straight ahead, not daring to lose her composure by glancing at Miriam. "I didn't do anything," she replied.

There was silence around the table.

Miriam looked insulted by the girls' remark, and her pretty and delicate face suddenly appeared painted and hard. "There is a rule in this house," she observed. "The children are not to close the doors to their rooms. Everyone knows this. There is a reason for this rule. And what is it?"

The question was answered by another swing of the kitchen door as Mariella came out searching for empty plates. A quick survey of the table, however, with its half-eaten food, the silence, and the unusual rigidity in the children's backs, convinced her that she had stepped into a scene. She nodded deferentially to the Señora and quickly departed. Tommy heard her whispering in the kitchen.

"The reason," continued Miriam with a quick glance toward the door, "is that it is unhealthy to hide things. Right, Peter?"

Her husband, caught off-guard by the procedural question, replied with a show of benevolence. "Well, uh, yes. It's certainly not healthy for us to hide things from one another. It breaks up the closeness of the family. That's why I'm always asking what we've done today and experienced. It's very important."

"There is no such thing as a secret in this house," continued Miriam with finality. "It's a very terrible thing for a child to hold in—a secret." She looked briefly into Tommy's eyes. "But—while I was in the garden—a secret was going on downstairs. Katy's door was closed. What was happening in there—for an hour? What kind of secret would a fifteen-year-old girl have that she doesn't want to share with us? Well?"

Miriam did not look at Katy all this time. She made her case impersonally, playing both prosecutor and judge. The rest of the court was passive. Katy herself did not look to anyone for support, and none of the children looked directly at her: it would imply too much of a conspiracy between them, and pass around the guilt. Tommy couldn't understand what Miriam was up to, for much as they shared a secret of their own, she apparently didn't intend to reveal it. Despite his sympathy for Katy, his primary emotion was relief that he hadn't been singled out himself. He even became curious about why Katy had closed the door.

"I wasn't doing anything. Nothing."

"Oh? Nothing? You were the person who closed the door—no? You knew the rule about keeping the doors open—no?"

"Yes."

"And yet you closed the door for no reason at all. It's strange that you closed the door for nothing. I would think you had a reason of some kind. Perhaps you do not like to have much to do with us. Or perhaps you have something to hide. A secret."

The girl blushed with bewilderment. Her eyes were moist, but still she did not dare look at anyone—it would only reveal how helpless she felt. "I wasn't doing anything. Dad!"

"Well, maybe she was just..."

"Don't make appeals to your father. There are rules in this house," continued Miriam more lightly. "If we go behind each other's backs it will be more difficult to enforce them, no?" She gave Mr. Montovan an affectionate look of reassurance.

"That's true. There are rules, now." He looked ahead thoughtfully with his face screwed up in great concentration. He was apparently considering, in a wise and thorough manner, the subtleties of the rules of the house, and for some reason the effort was quite painful to him.

"And the question remains: what was she doing in her room?" Miriam let the matter hang accusingly; then an airy playfulness lifted her face, reigned in by some secret intelligence. She finally deigned to look fully at her stepdaughter. Part of what made Katy look so vulnerable was that she was wearing a dress more appropriate for a twelve year old, with all kinds of silly frills. The girl continued staring at her plate, and murmured:

"I just closed the door. I was writing a letter."

"Ah, a letter! Really! There's a big difference between a 'letter' and a 'nothing.' It's interesting how a secret can lead to a lie." Miriam mused on the idea and looked at Tommy with insinuating eyes. Then she abruptly returned her attention to Katy: "I think we have something to talk about," she observed matter-of-factly.

"I want you to come down to my room after dinner."

"Yes, Miriam," said Katy.

With the end of the attack a semblance of peace returned to the table. The truce was dominated once again by the sound of forks and knives scraping against the plates, followed by munching and swallowing. There was an extraordinary amount of observation going on, whether it was the children peeping at Miriam, or the three boys covertly watching their sister for signs of tears. Katy looked at no one, maintaining a rigid composure, though surely aware that her brothers were stealing glances at her. Mr. Montovan kept a judicious eye throughout the proceedings, meaning, as far as the children were concerned, that he was neutral. Miriam continued eating her food, seemingly absorbed in the subtleties of its flavors and the intricacies of her own thoughts. Every so often, however, she studied Tommy. Her attention made the boy fidget, for he knew that by an act of omission she had put him in her debt. What puzzled him most was that there was no hardness in Miriam's face when she watched him anymore, only a kind of chagrin.

Hearing nothing from the kitchen but the din of pots clanging under the rushing water in the sink, Tommy wondered if Rafael and his wife were communicating with signs. In any case they must have been alert to any variations in the sounds coming from the dining room, for once the scraping of utensils against plates diminished significantly, Rafael appeared. He stood by the swinging door at the ready; and with no objection from the Señora, assessed that the meal was finished and began retrieving the empty plates. With a nod to the Señora he went back to the kitchen.

He and his wife returned momentarily with dessert. As usual it was rhubarb pie; a once tasty treat that was served so often and predictably that downing it was now a chore. Tommy continued glancing at Katy as he worked at his pie, its sour aftertaste more pronounced than usual. Katy ate more slowly than the others, and was playing with the crust when the three boys got up and excused themselves. Tommy made a point of passing near his sister as he swung around the table and said, "See ya, Katy."

"'Bye, Tommy," replied the girl softly. She didn't look up from her plate, and used her fork rather heavily to cut another bite. Tommy noticed that Miriam was leaning back in her chair observing the girl, and again wondered why Miriam chose to go after Katy instead of him. He walked downstairs feeling worried and confused.

Chapter Eight

From the desk in his room Tommy heard a chair scraping the floor; then the footsteps of his father walking to the den. Moments later other chairs moved followed by the sharper clicks of Miriam's heels and the soft padding of Katy behind her. Miriam led the girl downstairs. They paused halfway down the steps: perhaps Miriam was turning around to check on the girl; it was impossible to know. Otherwise her steps had a stately regularity. Once she arrived at the lower floor she led Katy directly to the master bedroom at the end of the hall. The door closed.

Tommy heard nothing for a long time. The silence made him even more curious about the interrogation two doors away, and he became acutely aware of irrelevant sounds coming from upstairs. Mariella, with none of the subtlety she had displayed when serving dinner, made a racket cleaning up the table and bringing everything to the kitchen. Plates sloshed as they were dumped in a sink of water, and there was more noise as the leftovers were put away. Then a few sharp words ensued between cook and wife; the argument seemed to fade without any resolution. Rafael started up again. "I don't know what shelf I put the cream in. If it's in the refrigerator, it's in the refrigerator, who cares where? You're always harping on order, order, order. If it's still fresh tomorrow, it's still fresh tomorrow. So dig around for it if you want!"

There was no immediate reply except for the angry crack of

a cabinet door closing. With the point made, the tiff dissipated and both went about their duties.

A few minutes passed before anything intelligible came from the bedroom. Then, gradually, Tommy made out the sound of Miriam's voice rising, culminating in: "I'm talking about lies!"

"No!"

"Oh?" came the reply. There was nothing distinct again: a few murmurs, accompanied by gaps of silence and further murmuring. Every so often Tommy made out the word "secret." "Secret" this, "secret" that; more silence.

"No!"

Tommy looked over at Billy. His brother was sitting alertly on his bed, picking out every possible word down the hall. Richard was standing in the doorway of his room across the hall. The boy wondered if even the servants were trying to follow the inquisition, for there was no more noise in the kitchen. He pictured his father reading in the den oblivious to it all.

"No!"

"Oh? A fifteen-year-old girl who has nothing to hide? Oh?"

There was silence again, followed by the word Miriam seemed to favor so much: "secrets." After awhile there came the faintly audible sound of Katy crying. Whether she was crying because Miriam had hit upon something, or simply because she was being attacked, was hard to say. Her sobs came in fits and starts, as though she were trying to hold them back. But she was unsuccessful, breaking down repeatedly, then quieting down and being humiliated into crying some more. It went on for ten minutes. There was another period of silence, then Miriam lecturing the girl, though the words were not distinct. A resolution occurred, or at least Miriam appeared satisfied with what had taken place, because the door opened once more.

There was one last direction from Miriam. Then Katy walked mechanically to her own doorway and hesitated; heading directly for the bathroom instead, where she closed the door. The faucet over the sink came on, followed by a very liberal splashing of water. Tommy heard Katy rummaging with a towel, and the door opened again. He stuck his head out of the room and saw her emerge with a sad, composed expression. Her face was red. She approached Tommy purposefully, but without looking at him directly, and once she got to his room glanced down the hallway before stepping inside.

"Well? What happened?" asked Tommy.

The girl peered out the doorway again as if being followed, then looked searchingly at her brother. Her eyes dropped. "She wants to see you, Tommy."

"Why?!"

"I don't know." She looked up again. Her eyes were bloodshot and she had to blink a few times. Her face had a questioning expression, and Tommy couldn't tell whether she wondered at something that he might have done or simply worried about whether he could bear up under their stepmother's scrutiny. There was great compassion in her eyes, but also restraint, as if she realized that pity was of no use.

"She said *now*, Tommy," Katy murmured. She led her brother out by the arm, and walked beside him in a plodding way as they went down the hall. When they got to her own doorway Katy became suddenly alert, and with a fearful glance down the hall, pulled the boy into her room.

"Be careful, Tommy!" she said urgently. "She's in a strange mood tonight." Katy looked him fully in the eyes, then an expression of helplessness came over her and she turned her face away. "Now go."

Despairing of learning more from his sister, Tommy took in the animal figurines from their mother's childhood on the dresser as a last solace, and retreated from the room. As he walked down the hall he prayed: "Oh, please God, don't let Miriam do anything to me. Make her leave me alone. Please let me be safe. Please, please, please." He didn't ask himself what safety there was in the world without his mother. He didn't really know.

For a moment he felt that Jesus was next to him and he wouldn't be alone; but that feeling dissipated once he reached Miriam's room. There was nothing particularly threatening about it. If anything, one's first impression was that there was something very casual about how things were thrown around. The dresser was littered with magazines and pill bottles; everywhere else articles of clothing were strewn about as if the wearer had a habit of changing suddenly. It was a great contrast to the cleanliness and order mandated in the rest of the house, and this contradiction made the boy uncomfortable. Otherwise the place was cozy and attracted the cats. Tommy counted three of them immediately, sprawled about much like the discarded clothes, in odd positions, and apparently very snug. The boy also noticed some of his father's and Miriam's underwear thrown over the back of the chair: and with that discovery he became aware of the mingled smell of cologne and perfume, which he strictly associated with adult privileges.

"So you found me. I was beginning to wonder where you were." The challenge in Miriam's voice seemed to come purely out of habit, for her manner was extremely relaxed. She was in an armchair facing the foot of the huge bed smoking a cigarette. She had apparently been thinking about something patiently, and the boy's entrance was neither expected nor an intrusion. She eyed him with distant curiosity and told him to sit down.

The only place to sit was at the foot of the bed, and Tommy did so hesitantly, knowing that his feet would barely touch the floor and that he would have nothing to lean back against. The mattress was so soft he was going to have to balance himself constantly with his hands; otherwise he would teeter one way or the other. Yet since he did not want to feel comfortable in that room, part of him welcomed the seesawing—it forced him to stay alert. The atmosphere in the room was so casual it was hard to imagine that the woman he was facing had been probing his sister mercilessly only moments before.

"Do you know why I asked you here?" asked Miriam, holding the cigarette elegantly between her fingers. "I think we have come to an understanding of sorts. Or will shortly." She inhaled a long puff. She held the smoke in her lungs for a moment, and then exhaled with cool deliberation. "I wanted to talk to you about some things. Some things the other children might not understand."

Being singled out in this way made Tommy uneasy, and though he tried to maintain a blank expression, a furrow appeared on his forehead and he looked away from her eyes. Miriam noted his expression but did not challenge it directly. It was an effective tactic, for when she inhaled again and blew smoke toward the ceiling, Tommy glanced back at her face. It was hard not to be curious about the intelligence animating her expression, and as she fell into her own thoughts she looked vulnerable.

"You haven't said anything," she broke in finally. "No, that's all right. You don't have to say anything yet. I wanted to talk about something special tonight. Actually a few things. For instance." The word 'instance' came out a little too harshly, and Miriam checked herself, pausing to take another drag as she considered the best way to proceed.

"How long have I been married to your father?" she asked.

"More than a year."

"More than a year? Closer to two, I would think." The edge in her voice was again unintended, and Miriam frowned at herself. "I've been married to your father for almost two years now. Two years. And it hasn't been particularly easy for me these two years. Do you know what I'm talking about?"

"Nuh-uh."

"No?" She looked at him sharply, but whatever temptation she had to seize on his answer faded away. "I mean that I'm not liked here—particularly."

This last statement seemed very dangerous to respond to, and

Tommy furrowed his eyebrows again and gripped the coverlet of the bed. Miriam's voice had a way of changing, even within a sentence, between a note of understanding and one of irony, and the possibility of threat behind her opening was not lost on the boy.

"No, not very much," she resumed. "And do you know why?" She looked him over carefully, and again he was too frightened to respond. She didn't press the issue. "Because I've tried to apply discipline on this household. Oh, yes. I knew it wasn't the popular thing to do. Not with the way your mother raised you."

Tommy felt a surge of anger at the insult, and glared at her without thinking of the consequences.

"I've had my reasons for this, and contrary to what you might think they are not selfish ones. Oh, no. Your father and I discussed this." She watched him coolly as the reference to her legitimacy sunk in. "We discussed what the best response was to this sudden loss—of their mother—for the children. And we decided in terms of what would be best for all of you in the long term."

Miriam smiled at him. "Actually," she continued, "I have a confession to make to you. My methods have not always been the most appropriate under the circumstances. I admit that. But my motive—that is not the question. My motives have been the right ones. Sometimes, however, I admit I have been harsh."

Tommy considered whether such a confession was difficult for her, but her manner was as casual as ever, her tone deliberate and flat. "Do you—have you—thought my treatment of you rather harsh sometimes?"

"Sometimes," replied the boy uncomfortably.

"Yes." She looked him over, but it was apparently the correct answer. "Strange. Strange the effect it has, no?"

She seemed to be murmuring almost entirely to herself, but it was the first thing she said that drew any sympathy from the boy. Her eyes became distant, and as she took another couple of drags, a strange sadness came over her features. She finally looked quizzically over what was left of her cigarette, and crushed it out.

"Do you want a coke?" she asked suddenly.

Tommy was so surprised by the question that he could only nod in response. Miriam got up confidently and walked over to a night table on the side of the bed. She pressed a buzzer on the wall behind the lamp and sat down again. That gesture had the immediate effect of changing the distant background noise from upstairs. There was a rustling in the kitchen; then Rafael's footsteps descended the back staircase to the servants' quarters. He opened the door from that secluded part of the floor, and approached the master bedroom down the hallway past the other children. By the time he arrived Miriam had lit another cigarette and crossed her legs; she was wearing an expression of dreamy patience. She recognized the cook presently by saying, "Could you do me the favor of bringing a coke for Tommy? And a whiskey-and-sour for me. Thank you, Rafael."

The cook nodded with grim politeness and glanced anxiously at the boy. He retreated without making up his mind about the situation, and his steps returned more quickly to the kitchen than they had come. Miriam blew out another stream of smoke, adding to the bitter haze that filled the room..

It was apparent that the conversation would go no further until the drinks arrived, and as far as Tommy could tell there was little anticipation in his stepmother's features. He tried passing the time glancing around the room, but couldn't help studying Miriam instead. He knew she had some design on him, but her mystery and undeniable prettiness still attracted him. He felt ashamed of his interest in her, but when she caught him staring, a smile came over her that was so genuine his heart almost opened up. There was amusement in the smile, and on almost anyone else the expression would be a sign of kindness and sympathy. But Tommy had the feeling there was only playfulness behind her smile, as well as an undercurrent of triumph. She looked away with unusual tact, but the amusement stayed with her as if she were balancing the feeling exquisitely in her mind.

Rafael returned shortly with a tray, and paused in the doorway until Miriam acknowledged him. He went to her first, bending forward gravely as she picked up her drink. Then he turned to the boy and his face brightened with an obvious and sincere effort as he said, "Ah! And a drink for the young man. And a good-night." The boy thanked him, and again the cook paused in the doorway until a nod from Miriam let him go. She took a subtle pleasure in the ceremony, and craned her head to watch him leave. Her eyes fell accidentally on the boy as she picked up her drink. "Go ahead," she said disarmingly.

Tommy lifted the cool glass and sipped from it. The ice in both drinks moved simultaneously with a tinkling that seemed conspiratorial in nature. Tommy became more relaxed and actually wondered if Miriam meant to make up to him in some way. The hopeful part of his nature felt the desire to be loved, and with it he worried about betraying his mother.

"I used to drink a lot of cokes," Miriam confided. "Now I drink—these. You become an adult." She looked Tommy over carefully, then inhaled from the cigarette, and let her face show a twinge of disappointment before exhaling another stream. "Well: I haven't always done the best thing here. That's what I was getting to. Funny to admit that, no?"

"Yes."

"Yes," repeated the woman. "I thought, maybe, by explaining a few things to you we might arrive at an understanding. An understanding for everyone in the family. Something you might help me communicate to the other children. I thought you might be able to help me in this way." She leaned toward Tommy, smiling, and evidently sensing his alarm at being trapped, leaned back again, eyeing him warily. Then she seemed to be pinched by pain and looked away. "When your father asked me to marry him, shortly after your mother passed away, I accepted. I loved your father. We had known each other well for some time.

So I was acquainted with the situation that presented itself. The responsibilities. I knew he had children. Of course there are certain ways to raise children correctly, if you take your responsibilities seriously."

Miriam spoke in a manner that combined detachment with an effort at sincerity. She seemed unsure how to proceed and sat back in the chair with her eyes focused on the smoke streaming from the cigarette. Her confusion, affected or not, made her more appealing to the boy as he watched her groping through her own artifice.

"Your mother was very soft on you children. Not a strict mother at all. She was rather—lackadaisical. I'm not saying she didn't care for you, of course—quite the contrary. But she was lackadaisical. Do you know what that means?"

The boy nodded sullenly.

"Hmm. You don't like what I'm saying. Do you, Tommy?"

"No," muttered the boy.

Miriam appraised him and seemed satisfied by the answer. "No. You're loyal. Of course you wouldn't want anyone to say anything bad about your mother. Of course not. But do you really think I would say anything to turn you against your mother? Well, Tommy?" The edge on the last two words did not appear to be accidental.

"No."

"Of course not." She relaxed again. "I'm only talking about her methods. But I do not think, whatever her intentions, that she was raising you properly. Do you have any idea what your reputation was, as a family, before I came into the picture?"

"No."

"You were considered brats. Out of control. Completely spoiled. Other people said that. People from the embassy. Yes. And how do you think you would have turned out if things had gone on like that—with no discipline?"

Tommy gripped the coverlet and said what his conscience told him to say. "She was a good mother."

This did not bother Miriam at all; she seemed encouraged by this minor act of rebellion. "Of course she was. But do you think her methods were the best for turning you into the sort of person you want to become? Or did you want to be a brat forever?"

"She was a good mother," repeated Tommy.

"Your father agreed with me on this, you know," Miriam said. She took her time crushing out the current cigarette. "We discussed it. And now you are—well-behaved kids. Other people notice this. At embassy functions we're complimented on your politeness. You should be proud of that. Do you think it would have helped your father's career, with the prominent position he has, to have children who were poorly behaved? Well?"

"No."

"I'm just making a point," she observed, as a note of warmth crept back into her voice. "But we're not just talking about politeness. That was not my primary motive. We are talking about preparing you for life as adults. It is not the sort of world out there that children raised softly can endure—not for long, anyway. Do you think it's a world out there of sweetness and light? Well, Tommy?"

"No?" said the boy, since it seemed to be the only safe answer.

"No. Quite the contrary." Miriam seemed deflated by her own reply. "It is world where terrible things happen. Where people can be quite cruel. You will learn that as an adult. "

The depiction of the adult world as a hard and lonely place was familiar to Tommy and it frightened him. He began thinking of his toys.

"We all do terrible things—sometimes," said Miriam, with a probing look at the boy. "No?"

Tommy did not reply, and nervously picked up his coke. The ice tinkled again.

"I just had your sister in here for a discussion," she noted sternly. "Do you know why?"

"Nuh-uh."

"I think you do. It's because she lied." The severity of her expression evaporated as she brushed a strand of hair away from her cheek. "Not a major lie, but a lie nonetheless. It's the principle of it. A small lie leads to a big lie. And every lie is dishonest. It ruins the character. I was quite harsh with her. Do you want your sister to grow up to be a—lying person?"

"No." Tommy couldn't think of anything else to say, but felt manipulated. He suspected that Miriam was trying to win approval for how she had treated the girl.

"Another effect of your mother's influence. But I won't go into that," continued Miriam with a show of exasperation. "I've done my best to lead her in the right direction."

She lit another cigarette, and a white Persian took the opportunity to jump on her lap. Tommy was always surprised at how the animals were drawn to her, and wondered if they were aware of something in her character that escaped him. She stroked the cat with her free hand, and a musing smile came over her. But after she began smoking the cigarette her thoughts seemed to collect themselves in a different order, as if something inside her had crumbled. At moments like these, when her face filled with shadows, the shallowness of her copper eyes was a real mystery.

"I did all this out of love, you know," she said. "You may not believe it, but it was love. Not that careless sort of love you expected from your mother. I have tried to act responsibly. I realized it would not be popular, but that small sacrifice on my part was in order for the sake of your future. You will understand when you are an adult. You will thank me then." She took a thoughtful drag off the cigarette and glanced at the boy before breaking into a laugh. "You must be thinking, 'What strange things she is telling me! What strange behavior!' But it hasn't been easy for me—do you think? Being the mean one all the time. Being disliked. Ha!" Then she added in a softer voice, "But I have my needs too. Do you understand what it has been like for me these two years, being—hated—when I am only trying to do what is right? When it is done out of love? Don't you think I deserve to be loved back?"

"Yes," said Tommy, fiddling with the drink. He decided reluctantly that she was probably right; and that God really had sent her to improve his character.

"I thought you would understand. Of all the children," she said. "But—oh—here comes your father."

Mr. Montovan entered the room hastily to look for some papers, and was surprised to see Tommy sitting on the bed.

"Your son and I are having a—conversation," announced Miriam with exquisite delicacy.

"I can see that. Hello Tommy." Mr. Montovan put his hands in his pockets and studied the boy gravely.

"Hi, Daddy."

His father looked troubled by something, but, apparently remembering the papers, lifted them off the dresser and left the room.

"He's gone now," said Miriam, as if they were sharing a joke. "Are you enjoying your coke?"

"Uh-huh."

She raised her whiskey in salute, and the ice in both glasses clinked in a slow whirl. "Have you anything to say?"

"I think I'm lucky to have such a pretty stepmother," he blurted out. "And that—I'm lucky you want me to be better." In the back of his mind he felt uneasy about what he'd said, and what his mother would think of him.

"Yes," said Miriam with satisfaction. She lifted the hand she had been using to pet the cat and adjusted her wig. "Thank you." As she studied the boy her face became more alert and hard. She sat back to consider something and inhaled from the cigarette. "We had an interesting experience in the garden today, didn't we?" she asked.

"What?"

"Ha! Now don't act so innocent, Tommy," she returned lightly. "Really. It's the same complaint I had about your sister—lying. It really runs in you children, doesn't it? Now you know and I know what you did."

"I didn't do anything."

She laughed. "There you go again," she said. "Now tell me one thing. Do you think you can fool me? I mean, really. This is between you and me."

Tommy made an effort to look in her eyes. "No," he replied.

"No," she said with a smile. "Of course not. But you certainly are trying. I must say I admire your technique, Tommy. Really. I mean it certainly works with your father, doesn't it? But it doesn't work with me. Oh, I wonder what goes on in your little mind sometimes, that little mind of yours. Clever Tommy. Very clever Tommy. No, I see right through you, you know. All the time. Don't you forget it."

She spoke with breezy authority, and when she was done, shrugged her shoulders. "Now—do me a favor. Won't you? Tell me the truth. What did happen between you and that little shepherd boy?"

The openness in Miriam's face implied that he only had to be honest to be her friend, and the contract between them would be sealed. Even the combination of amiability and heartlessness in her manner appealed to the boy because her approach seemed to contain elements of justice. It was unwise to cross the woman sitting so close to him, who apparently had all the right intentions, because she would rule over him until he was a grown man. Yet something about her repelled him utterly. And the momentum of the lie held him back, for much as he wanted to let it go, the lie was bound up perversely with his integrity now.

"I didn't do anything. I wouldn't do anything to hurt a boy like that."

Miriam looked startled, but the shock gave way quickly to an expression of wonder and even respect. Finally she just looked embarrassed. "Whatever," she said dismissively, as she flicked the ash off the cigarette. On second thought she simply crushed the whole thing out and put the ashtray aside. "But I must have you consider the consequences of what you've done. I'm sure you have thought about them already. You may have. You have a conscience of your own, I'm sure. Think about this. That boy has quite a scar on his face. Oh, yes. He did not have a very good doctor. He will always have that scar. He will live with it. And you are responsible. You. You will live with it as well. " She pushed the Persian off her lap and brushed a few hairs from her skirt.

"However. This will remain between you and me. I will not tell anyone else what you've done, as long as we have—an understanding. Do you know what that is?"

Tommy shook his head.

"Hmm. You will remember what I've told you. You will try to tell this to the other children. When it is—natural. Do you know what I'm saying?"

"Uh-huh."

"That I have used these methods out of love. I would like them to understand that." She began looking confused, and from the nervous movements of her hands, floating from the sides of her armchair to her lap, it was obvious she wanted to light another cigarette, though she refrained from doing so. Her face stiffened.

"I would like you to tell me how they react. Be honest. Tell me what they say. Tell me—what they think of me, if they have any doubts. Keep me informed. For their sakes. Can you do that?"

The boy looked at his feet. He did not feel secure at the edge of the bed.

"Undoubtedly you will at least consider it," said Miriam ironically. Then she seemed to realize she had gone too far, and her face softened with doubt. She did not say anything for a while.

"How do you feel now, Tommy?"

"Not very good."

"Hmm. Well there is only one thing to do about it, isn't there?"

"What?"

"Hug me."

Tommy looked into her face and she arched an eyebrow playfully. "Oh, I won't eat you up. Come on. It'll make you feel better. And me too." Her arms fell away from her lap to make space for him.

"Okay." The boy blinked a few times, covered the space between them in two steps, and slipped his arms above her waist. She was surprisingly soft. She put her arms around his shoulders and he tightened his grip until he felt her heartbeat through the palm of his hand. Miriam held him lightly, with no real pressure, but a definite air of possession. She sighed in her pleased and amused way, and as Tommy felt the bristles of her wig tickling his cheek, he thought of the differences between real and fake hair. Her perfume was pleasant and light, but mingled with the bitter residue of smoke.

"There—that feels better—no? Your mother held you like this, didn't she?"

"Uh-humm."

"It's easy, isn't it? No? To have an understanding. When I was a girl, my mother held me like this. We were quite close. It was pleasant." Miriam sighed abstractedly. "It should always be this way, shouldn't it?"

"Uh-huh."

"Mmm. My mother was very consistent. I appreciate that now," She said, more to herself. "Which brings me to another point. A problem." She said nothing more after that, and the boy, who was just beginning to relax, felt deeply alarmed. He also noticed something odd about her hug, for, soft as her arms were, they lay limply on his shoulders.

"What?" he asked finally.

Miriam considered some more, and then, without any real use of strength, moved her arms, gripped him on the shoulders, and pushed him away so that she could look him fully in the face.

"You lied," she said wearily. "Oh, don't look away, you know it's true. I was on to you from the start, Tommy. Don't give me any of those innocent looks. I was hoping you would volunteer the information on your own. I was—disappointed. I know perfectly well what you did to that Indian boy. You are quite as capable of cruel things as anybody. I see that in you." Her face became very grave. "Don't worry. I will keep my part of the bargain. I will not tell anyone what you've done. You would not like that, no? But I must punish you for lying to me. I will be consistent, that I will promise you. But we will get on much better if you are honest with me. Now take down your pants."

"No, Miriam. Please."

"*Now*. Really, Tommy," she said with disappointment. She stood up, and once more brushed cat hairs from her skirt. "Now."

"*Please*, Miriam."

"Jesus in Heaven! Who do you think you are?!" she replied. "Do it."

The boy turned away toward the closet so that he wouldn't be facing her, and with trembling hands unbuckled his belt. Then he undid the button to his pants and pulled down the zipper. Miriam watched disinterestedly as the pants fell to the floor.

"That's a start. Good. Now face the bed."

Tommy obeyed and looked down at the coverlet. "Please, Miriam," he tried once more. "Please don't do it. I won't be bad again. I promise."

"Please, please, please," she replied coolly. "The thing to do is get it over with. Really. You will thank me for this when you are an adult, I assure you. I am doing you the favor of being consistent. You *may* even thank me tomorrow." She walked lazily over to the closet and opened the door as if she were looking for nothing in particular. She removed one of the worn leather belts belonging to her husband and walked back to the bed. "Your underpants, too," she said, observing him professionally. "Now bend over."

She doubled up the belt and tested it by whacking the top of the mattress suddenly. This startled all the cats, the Persian particularly, who had found a very comfortable spot under the bed. He bolted out of the room in a streak of white fur, causing Miriam to glance at the door with consternation. Then she took notice of the boy again and sighed.

"Now, Tommy," she exclaimed, with a mixture of amusement and irritation. "Don't cover your fanny with your hands. It'll just make things worse."

Chapter Nine

In the morning Chaco awoke with a queasy feeling, remembering the Indian kids crossing the plateau the day before. The light coming in through the stalks of the hut was diffuse and gray; and when he slipped outside before the others awoke he saw that a cloud had settled into the valley overnight. It was thrilling to have a cloud for such a close neighbor, for despite the fact that the boy had spent every night of his life on that slope he was still awed by the lurking power of low clouds, and their capriciousness.

He decided to collect some rocks. It wasn't easy to find them near the hut since the packed dirt there had been swept by generations of passing feet, but further along the path to the main road there were plenty. He selected rocks with sharp edges that were small enough for the slingshot he used to kill birds. The boy hoped that the slingshot and a few good stones were adequate protection from the gang, that the mere sight of him holding the weapon would turn them away. If only he had had it the day the gringos came! There was no defense against laughter, however, and it was the mocking laughter of the drunken kids and the gringo's mother that chilled him the most.

Chaco filled his pockets and made sure to cover the bulges with his poncho. He walked back toward the hut. Though he had only been gone a few minutes the low cloud was already dissipating under the early sunlight. His father was in the doorway looking out for him and turned back inside at his approach.

Chaco noticed a grasshopper perched on the packed dirt beside the hut, apparently stunned by the want of vegetation.

He received a breakfast of two pieces of stale bread with a cup of coffee. He ate without enthusiasm, dreading the journey uphill. He would be alone and vulnerable all day—and to what? What was implied in the laughter that frightened him so much? He stole a few glances at Sylvia, but her carefree manner told him she didn't remember what he'd confided to her the day before. He stoically decided not to remind her.

Achuale slung on a machete over his shoulder for work at a neighboring ranch, took a cloth bag from his wife, and patted the boy on the head as he left. It was a sign of Chaco's maturity that he and his father went to work separately now, and received the same lunch. His mother handed him his own bag, filled with a small cup of lima beans, a jar of water, and more bread. Then she quickly pulled him into an embrace and pushed him toward the door.

He picked up the staff leaning against the shack and his sister followed him to the pen. She opened the gate to the enclosure with great ceremony, watching playfully as the sheep ambled out. Then she swung the gate shut, waved at her brother, and headed back to the shack.

Chaco noticed that she still made no reference to his fears and seemed supremely confident of his ability to handle himself. It made him feel proud and lonely. As he watched her go inside he noticed that while the cloud in the valley was almost gone, another was looming heavily just above the hut. It was in no hurry to go anywhere; it too would become a victim of the direct sun.

The sheep began looking confused, and Chaco stamped the staff a few times and called to the dog. It was remarkable how urgently the mongrel went to its work! After he ran around the flock yapping, the sheep formed a loose column and followed the path through the corn towards the dirt road. The boy couldn't help looking back a few times at the new cloud as currents of air passing between the hills shaped it languidly into a longer puff.

The boy wondered what gave the dog its energy. He considered what scraps the animal had for breakfast, and though he had no particular sympathy for the dog, he admired the enthusiasm the creature brought to his job. Of everyone advancing along the path, only the dog assumed that his efforts had purpose, were appreciated by his masters—and were fun. Chaco envied its stupid happiness and took a last look at the cloud in the valley. It was nothing more than a wisp.

They reached the paved road. He chased the sheep uphill, yelling "Hui! Hoo!" and then slowed down again, letting them get ahead a few yards as he caught his breath. Then he resumed the march behind them, always conscious of the rocks jiggling in his pockets. Fear came over him whenever he thought about reaching the plateau. Yet what was there to be afraid of? Only the laughter he heard the day before; and as he watched the changing sky he realized what it was about the laughter that worried him so much. It was the implication that his duties were meaningless—a joke; that all his effort for his family would come to nothing; that he was nothing. Ha! Ha! Ha! It was the kind of taunt that the mongrel, trotting so officiously beside the flock, was oblivious to.

As they approached the wealthy neighborhood Chaco's eye was caught by another small cloud hovering just above the roofs. It behaved like an intimate, otherworldly neighbor, but it too was drifting away, like the other low clouds, to a more detached position over the center of the city in the great valley below him. Why did the clouds move further away as the morning became bright? It was a mystery the boy never tired of; yet he felt there was something terribly impersonal about it. In his melancholy mood even the weather was a little frightening.

Chaco paused, as he usually did, across from the gringo's house, and tried to imagine what life was like inside. Not much could be seen through the windows this time of morning, and the workings of the place remained inviolate. Yet somewhere in the house was the boy who cut his cheek and the woman who laughed at him so mockingly. Why were they allowed to get away with it? Finally an older servant woman came on the deck to shake out a rug, and when she began studying him with particular interest, he prodded the sheep to go on.

Chaco and the animals took their customary route through the construction sites just as the guards were coming on watch. The sun had still not risen over the top of the mountain, and it was seemingly the reward of the flock for climbing the whole distance to be blinded by it the moment they reached the plateau. Only there, under the full glare of the morning, was it obvious how filthy and gray the sheep's coats really were. Chaco couldn't help wondering how the sun changed the night clouds into brilliant puffs and had no effect whatsoever on the sheep.

The morning was uneventful. Chaco took his supply of thin ropes out of a bag he'd been carrying and spent a few minutes binding the sheep to their stakes, a job he did very efficiently now. He briefly considered whether to move the stakes into lusher grass, but decided to do it tomorrow. Then he found a rock to sit on and passed the time watching the sky.

It didn't take long, with the sun rising, for the weather to assume the austere qualities he was so accustomed to. The clouds floated higher or drifted over the city until they no longer had any neighborly quality and became utterly detached from terrestrial affairs. The sky was a very generous bright blue. It was the one element of the weather that gave Chaco comfort: everything else, beautiful as it was, made him feel lonely. From his perch on the boulder even the city looked toy-like and irrelevant to his problems.

Hours passed. The sheep grazed quietly on the short grass: the stakes really should have been moved over a few yards. The mongrel lay on the edge of the flock, taking no particular notice of the sheep and yet seemingly alert to any possible disturbance.

He was content. Perhaps if Chaco felt any sympathy for the animals he would have taken comfort in their presence and been assuaged of his fears. But that was beyond him, and he watched them essentially with indifference. As the sun rose to the middle of the sky, he ate the beans and drank the water his mother gave him, and threw a few scraps of bread to the dog.

Though Chaco never had a watch, he had discovered a regular and novel way to mark the time. Every fifteen minutes an airplane would land, or take off, from Quito International Airport. From his vantage on the rock he couldn't see the landing strip itself, but the rise and fall of the planes filled him with wonder. Where did they come from, and what were their destinations? He concluded that most came from that rich country to the north, bringing gringos to his own land. He watched as a great white airplane approached the runway with a dim roar from its jets. More gringos. What are they doing here? He wondered. He thought of the wealthy neighborhood below him, the boy with the rock, and his mother's laugh. He shivered.

After fifteen minutes a plane took off, heading northwest. How did it feel to fly so confidently into the sky? How much did it cost? Chaco pondered this, in awe of the gringos' freedom to soar from one place to the next and their exhilarating power to coast through the clouds. The gringos were even more powerful than the weather. And what had they done with this vast power of theirs? Cut his face open and humiliate him with laughter. He watched the plane disappear and felt a surge of anger: the gringos came and went as they pleased, abandoning problems; while he had to endure their insults, watch the sheep alone for the sake of his family—for nothing! Ha! Ha! Ha!

Most of the afternoon went uneventfully. Every so often Chaco got bored and hopped down from the boulder to wander along the fringes of the flock, kicking the grass. Occasionally, a determination would seize him, and he would practice shooting the rocks in his pockets at the boulders. He was careful to retrieve each one, reasoning that there was something special about the rocks near his house. But he still felt anxious, and was only partly reassured when he saw familiar Indians passing with their cattle to other parts of the plateau. Only in the late afternoon, while circling the pasture, did he notice the gang of kids who had mocked him the day before.

They were standing where the path went over the edge of the plateau, and seemed to be observing him. He wasn't sure how long they had been there. But they were obviously conferring about something, and every so often the tallest of the boys, apparently a teenager, pointed in his direction. He heard murmuring sounds. Was it laughter again? He made a pretense of not being interested in the other boys, but as he kicked the grass he would stop to look at them; and then quickly kick the grass again in a show of independence. After a while Chaco decided to sit on his boulder, and walked back to it as casually as he could.

The boys continued watching him. Then they began moving across the field. There was nothing in their behavior to distinguish it from yesterday's. They walked languorously, sweeping across the field in their brown ponchos, as if they had nowhere in particular to go, and nothing in particular to do, and were superior to other people because of that. They pointed to the shepherd boy every now and then and laughed. The mongrel pricked up his ears and watched the band without moving from his spot; Chaco clutched the rocks in his pockets. Then the boys simply walked out of sight.

Chaco relaxed, and for the first time all day felt truly grateful for the presence of the dog. He wondered where the kids had gone, and again thought about their laughter. He got up and walked around the sheep awhile. The mongrel followed him until he realized the boy was wandering in circles. An hour later the band of kids returned. Chaco was sitting on his boulder, and clutched the rocks in his pocket and the slingshot under his poncho. This time the boys swaggered past more closely than before and taunted him. "Shh...Look at him: the guardian angel—of sheep!" laughed the tallest kid. "Ha! Ha! Ha!" Chaco heard other descriptions as well: The "stupid," the "loser;" finally he was called "little ugly-face."

They passed so closely that the mongrel got up and barked; their response was more laughter and cries of "Mutt!" The kid at the end of the group picked up a pebble and threw it at the hide of a sheep. That was the end of the provocation. Chaco didn't feel the attack was serious enough to warrant retaliation (not when there were so many other boys), so he kept his weapon hidden, watching them rigidly as they swept over the edge of the plateau and disappeared down the path.

Chaco repeated "little ugly-face" to himself and felt the ridges of his scar, wondering how far away it was visible. Pretty far, most likely, he decided glumly. So that's how he was known among the other Indian kids. The idea was alien to him and it was hard adjusting to it. The dog trotted around the sheep triumphantly, assuming that his barks had kept the kids at bay, and the shepherd felt jealous of his happiness. Still, that was the end of the moment he had dreaded so much, and it wasn't nearly as bad as he had assumed. He felt such relief that he was even grateful to the Indian boys because their worst wasn't nearly as bad as the gringos.

And he had weathered it by himself. That was something to be proud of, and as he sat there, knowing he would never say anything about it to his father, Chaco felt he had taken another step toward maturity. It did not surprise him now that with every bit of growth his loneliness increased.

He watched as another plane lifted off from the airport, glinting hazily in the afternoon sun and accelerating with a roar. More gringos heading for the North. So many people with their destinies compressed together! What did the beautiful machine say to him as it took its distinguished passengers to their freedom? Ha! Ha! Ha! Ha! Ha! Ha! Why were they blessed with such fortunate lives while he was left on the mountaintop with his scar? Ha! Ha! Ha!

Fifteen minutes later a propeller plane, less graceful than the jets, landed with its passengers from the port of Guayaquil. He counted four more flights leaving and coming to the airport, and decided to go home a bit early. He was quite adept at untying the ropes to the sheep's legs, but his oppressive mood slowed him down. It would have been much easier if he could speak to his father about his troubles, but since that was out of the question he was left with the burden of explaining them to no one. What meaning did it have if he had to bear everything himself? Chaco freed the last of the sheep, and waved his staff mechanically to form them into a line.

The dog trotted along the head of the flock with his usual enthusiasm, barking to no apparent effect. The sheep were as apathetic as ever, and Chaco was less than diligent in urging them forward. He was thinking how familiar the path downhill was, how he had memorized almost every rock, recognizing them even in the stingy half-light by which he usually guided himself home. He followed the animals around the second big turn in the path and leaned against a boulder as he watched the progress of the sheep.

The boys were waiting for him on outcroppings along the trail. It looked as though they had been sitting for a while; and with their ponchos arrayed around them, might as well have been part of the boulders. The gang paid little attention to the passing of the sheep or the dog, but when Chaco approached they met him with stares. The tall kid, sitting on a ledge only five feet from the shepherd, leered at him as he flicked a cowlick away from his forehead. "Oh my! Here comes the angel of the sheep. Now what do you have to say to us, Canyon-face?"

At "Canyon-face" the rest of the kids laughed. This delightful description hadn't been floated before.

"I'm going home."

"Ha! Ha! He tells us he's going home. What a dutiful little boy. What is it, you don't like us, boy? Is he going home, my friends?"

Again there was laughter, a couple shouts of "No! He's coming with us!" and more chuckling. Chaco's chest tightened as he felt for the rocks and the slingshot.

"A nervous little runt," observed the tall one, who was obviously the leader. The cowlick fell again, and he brushed it away with contempt. "Where'd you get the cut, Canyon-face?"

"Some gringos did it," declared Chaco with a touch of pride. "I was sitting up there a couple of months ago watching the sheep, and they came up and attacked me with rocks."

The boy felt solidarity with the Indian boys and hoped that his revelation would earn their respect, but it was met for the most part with vacant frowns. The tall one regarded Chaco pensively, but his serious expression gradually changed into a mocking leer. "Ooh, he let the gringos cut his face open. How nice of him. How accommodating. Did you let them ram your ass too? Eh—Shepherd Boy?"

The gang considered the last remark exceedingly funny, and another chorus of laughter erupted, decaying into snorts. Chaco felt a wave of terror pass over him as he fingered the stones and the slingshot again. He knew they were useless.

"Silly boy. Why do you sit on that rock all day, watching sheep? Eh, Shepherd Boy?"

"Because I'm supposed to—for my family. They're my father's sheep."

The leader tilted his face. "He's a good boy, isn't he, friends?"

"Oh, yes! Oh, yes!"

"They're your father's sheep? You watch them for your father?"

The leader observed him without expression, then leaned forward and picked up a rock the size of his fist. He tossed it up once, weighing it in his palm, and evaluated the boy as a target. Chaco felt his courage sneaking away, but he put up a brave front, facing the older boy stiffly.

"They're your father's, eh?" asked the leader again.

"Yes."

The tall boy nodded, twisted around at his waist and threw the rock powerfully at the hindquarter of a sheep.

"Baa-aa!"

The sheep ran off the path a few paces, then stood in a daze, lifting its hind leg a couple of times. The tall boy looked back at Chaco with a sullen grin.

"Baa-aa!" belched another kid, who was seated on a lower rock than most of the gang and was obviously drunk. Once he was done, he didn't smile or laugh, but simply stared at Chaco with glazed eyes.

"That's 'Perfume'," said the leader. "Do you know why we call him 'Perfume'? Eh? Why is that, Perfume?"

The boy in question replied with a proud burp.

"Because he'll drink anything. Anything that makes him feel good. But perfume is the sweetest. Eh, buddy?"

Perfume removed a flask from under his poncho as a demonstration, opened the cap with great ceremony, and took a sip of the bright yellow liquid inside. Even from where Chaco stood it had a bracing, sickly-sweet smell. He burped again, put the flask away, and regarded Chaco with stolid triumph. His eyes were so dull he looked blind.

"Delicious, eh? Do you want to try some, Canyon-face? Huh?" laughed the tall boy. "Do you want to stay with us awhile?"

"I have to go home now," replied Chaco in a small voice. "I can't be very late. My parents are expecting me. I have to return the animals."

This was met with more laughter, which sounded better natured than before and made the boy a little more comfortable. But then the leader jumped off his seat and crossed his arms. Most of the others followed suit, encroaching into the path just enough to hinder Chaco's escape. The flock, released from the shepherd's discipline, was spreading out, and even the dog was getting confused. He trotted back along the sheep to check on his master, and stopped apprehensively when he saw so many boys on either side.

"Oh, please, *please* stay with us," implored the tall boy sarcastically. "We need someone like you *so* much." He paused for effect. "To scare away the birds! Ha! Ha! Ha!"

This was another extremely popular joke, with howls so loud the mongrel stepped back, scratched himself, and stood in a half-crouch with his ears down. Chaco felt another wave of terror, and was so beside himself he pulled his right hand out of his pocket to feel his scar.

"He touches it, he touches it, to see if it's there!" screamed a small kid at the back of the group. This led to the greatest howling of all, such that the mongrel, scared as he was, barked with tentative defiance.

"You have a doggie," observed the leader. He condescended to give the animal a glance, and then, seeing Chaco hide his hand, said, "Yes. And you have a big fat ugly scar, too. Do you know what that means?"

"No."

"It means the girlies aren't going to like you. No, the girlies aren't going to like you at all—if they can even bear to look. Have you thought about that, kid? Huh?"

Chaco couldn't bear to reply. Tears began welling in his eyes. He had a faint hope that his emotions weren't visible to the other boys, but he gave himself away when he blinked. As the tears streamed down his cheek the gang responded with inevitable whoops and howls. He hadn't considered the effect of the scar very far into the future, and his mother and sister were too kind to imply that it would affect the feelings of any girl. With everyone laughing at him, and as he watched the sheep wandering away from his control, it occurred to the boy that he might not marry.

The leader smiled maliciously as his cowlick fell over his forehead again. His face became disinterested, however, as he flicked it away. He had already humiliated Chaco a great deal, and his attitude hung in a balance between letting the shepherd go and humiliating him even more. Somewhat lazily he arrived at a decision.

"You work for the gringos," he declared flatly.

"I do not! That's not true! I work for my family!" replied Chaco.

"Everyone who works, works for the gringos," continued the leader evasively. "They control everything. Or the rich do. What's the difference?" He laughed hollowly and picked up a few pebbles.

What are the pebbles for? wondered Chaco. Everyone else in the gathering was curious about them as well, including the boy who held them in his palm. It was an idle gesture, picking them up; but as leader the older boy realized it mustn't seem to be wasted. He began tossing the little ones at Chaco's feet. Most of the throws were harmless as he chanted, "Little boy wants to go *home*! Little boy loves his *sheep*!" But a couple of times, as a kind of punctuation, he threw the rocks really hard at the boy's tattered boots and Chaco screamed.

The boys had stopped laughing, and even the leader was ashamed of himself, deciding the whole thing had gotten pointless. Then the dog barked suddenly to protect his master, and approached the group in a semi-crouch. The mongrel seemed to gain confidence after the first couple of barks, and began yapping continually, though he stopped a few feet away from the closest kids. His intervention had one immediate and beneficial effect: for the pelting of Chaco's feet stopped.

"You have a *doggie*," remarked the older boy maliciously. A couple of the kids glanced at the mongrel and chuckled.

The dog reacted by barking some more, but when it was obvious that Chaco was no longer crying his response became more tentative. He only barked occasionally and mostly out of confusion, because he was not sure what he was facing. The gang became more curious about the dog and the pressure on either side of the shepherd loosened. The mongrel barked once more out of fear. He noticed that Chaco was still standing in the middle of the other boys and did not know how to read his master's relationship to them. He quieted completely.

"You have a doggie-doggie," repeated the tall boy as he picked up a stone. He stepped into the middle of the path between the dog and his master. "He-ere, little dog! Here, mutt-mutt!"

The mongrel seemed surprised at the appeal. He twisted his head toward Chaco, looking for a signal to either come as he was told or run to safety. At first his master was too frightened to do anything more than stare back impassively. Then he softly commanded, "Go!"

The dog pricked up his ears, but did not understand.

"Here, dog-dog!" said the tall boy.

The dog stood very still, as if waiting for the scent a breeze would bring. Then he looked at Chaco, and receiving no signal from him, crept closer. A couple of the boys laughed and the dog stopped. The leader quieted them, and after another call of "Come, doggie!" the mongrel decided everything was all right and trotted a few steps more.

The leader threw the stone. It whizzed past the mongrel's snout, barely missing him, and bounced off the side of the path. The dog stopped immediately and crouched. His ears went down, his tail went between his legs, and the boys laughed.

"Ha! Ha! Ha! Ha! Ha!"

The dog stared at Chaco, confused by how stiffly the boy was standing and the lack of expression on his face. The other kids couldn't believe how silly the animal was, and realized they would be able to play with him some more.

"Here, doggie, doggie," insinuated the leader. He picked up another rock.

An awful feeling of helplessness came over Chaco. He did not care for the dog particularly, but the loyalty of this creature he rarely thought about moved him. Still, he felt paralyzed by the thought that the rock in the older boy's hand might end up smashing his face instead, and the horror of being struck by the gringo boys came back to him. "Go, go!" he muttered, louder than before, but not commandingly enough to overcome the dog's instinct to protect him.

The older boy weighed the rock, and looked over Chaco's smooth cheek as a warning. Then he bent forward toward the mongrel. "Here, doggie, doggie," he intoned with his free hand outstretched. The animal looked at the leader and quivered at his scent. Once more he looked at Chaco for guidance, but the boy was too frightened to respond. The dog stepped forward tentatively, then trotted toward his master.

The rock smashed into his foreleg with a crack.

"Aaar!" The dog yelped, then collapsed on his side breathing. He kept moving his head, trying to find Chaco, and finally twisted himself up with his good front leg. He gave the boy a dazed sidelong look, and sensing his betrayal, turned around and limped away as the other boys tossed pebbles at him. Perfume belched again with peculiar satisfaction.

"Ha! Ha! Ha! Ha! Ha!"

The sport was over. The leader of the boys, realizing he had taken the situation as far as it would go, put an ending on it that confused Chaco a great deal. The older boy watched the dog progress to a safe distance, then turned to the shepherd and announced magnanimously: "Let that be a lesson to your gringo friends. If we catch them messing with you again, we'll knock them like that—hah!"

"Split their heads open!" interjected a member of the chorus.

"Ha! Ha! Ha! Ha! Ha!"

Perfume burped once more and raised his flask.

"You can go home to your Papi now—Shepherd Boy," said

the leader with a sneer. Despite the contempt with which he spoke, he too raised his hand in a salute. The gang laughed, but as Chaco made his way through them, he felt a camaraderie with them and wondered whether the whole encounter had been an initiation.

The dog was sitting a few yards off the path a little further downhill, licking his leg. He had given up any effort to keep the flock together. Chaco did nothing to urge him on, but chased the fringes of the scattered flock himself, yelling "Hui!" and "Hoo!" It took fifteen minutes waving his staff to get the sheep in any order at all, and still the dog sat in an aloof daze. He started following the boy from a distance, limping badly, as Chaco led the flock toward the construction sites. The boy didn't know whether the mongrel's leg was broken or not, and felt too ashamed of himself to make up with the dog or check the injury. Whenever he looked back the dog stopped and eyed him warily.

For a while the boy derived a restless energy from his relief at not being hurt, and once again his attitude toward the boys was dominated by profound gratitude at being let go. Yet that mood dissipated quickly enough. The leader's taunts and his own betrayal of the dog made him anxious and depressed.

It was true that he was ugly. It was true as well that girls probably wouldn't like him, though Chaco no longer resented the other boy for saying so. He only knew that the stain on his future began on the day the gringo boy threw the rock. What was the cruelty of the Indians to his dog compared with that? He wondered if it was true as well that the gringos controlled everything. The audacity of the idea was difficult to absorb; then the roar of another jet rising above the hills distracted him. Of course they had the power to control everything: and with that thought the futility of his work became overwhelming. He suddenly felt distant from his family and father, and began to identify with the gang that had just frightened him. They were the only ones who promised to do anything about the gringos at all.

He walked downhill with a melancholy lassitude, occasionally bursting out with energy when he noticed the sheep scattering again. Then he would chase them back to a narrow file on the path, yelling constantly, uncomfortably aware of the rocks still banging around in his pockets. He really began missing the services of the dog. He started calling to him, but the mongrel, having abandoned any sense of duty, followed him cautiously on his three good legs. The boy began to suspect that the dog strung behind him only because he didn't know where else to go.

When they passed through the construction sites Chaco felt slightly better, if only because the surroundings were different from the open spaces where he faced so much trouble alone. It was still light enough to appreciate the fine fresh paint on the houses that were almost finished: soon this would be a neighborhood, and he would be an alien passing through it, not just a shepherd with a right-of-way. Manuel was watching from the roof of a grand house surrounded by piles of bricks. He waved noncommittally to the boy. There was something abnormal about the behavior of the flock with the limping sheep at the end of the line and the wounded dog barely keeping pace; Manuel had his suspicions about the gang of wild kids who had been hanging around recently. But to what purpose was any sympathy for the shepherd or speculations about what had happened above? Manuel had spent many months watching the comings and goings on the path and had many opinions about these various journeys. His loyalties, however, were to the paymaster who owned the plot of land and the materials he was sent to protect. What happened outside those boundaries, especially out of sight, he felt helpless to affect.

Chaco adjusted the sack with the ropes hanging on his shoulder and cried out to a wayward sheep. He cracked the staff against a boulder, and the animal, understanding the threat of punishment, fell into place immediately. The boy lapsed into his melancholy reveries, counting the bruises to his self-respect;

and the sheep inevitably began wandering. He was startled into action again. The pattern continued until they descended into the wealthy neighborhood and a new cloud caught his attention.

It was a low-flying cloud burning with warm and generous light from the departing sun. Was it merely a coincidence that it hovered above the gringo's house, or did it confer some of its temporary glory on the great establishment below? Chaco's fascination with clouds coupled with his memory of the house was enough to make him pause. It was impossible for him not to drop his prejudices and admire the beauty of the place for what it was. He felt small: for what was his love for his family, his problems, or his own troubled future compared to the magnificent house and the blessing conferred upon it by the low-flying cloud? He gazed wonderingly upon the sparkling fountains, the gleaming walls and the well-attended gardens. Then he noticed his adversary playing alone by the flowerbed along the fence. His eyes were caught by the gringo's golden hair, which seemed like another ornament blessing the property.

Segundo, who was bent over a row of geraniums by the deck, looked up and saw an Indian child gazing at the property from the other side of the road. It wasn't an unusual occurrence, but something about the boy troubled him. Perhaps it was the longing in the boy's face and the fact that nothing could be done to satisfy it. He was so uncomfortable that he left Tommy entirely to himself. He descended the steps to the back yard, thinking as he did so that Tommy had been limping rather strangely that afternoon.

Tommy didn't notice the other boy right away. He was playing very intently, to erase his memory of the night before, and to recapture the magic of the front flowerbeds from the time before the incident with the rock. He had admired the cloud himself as he came outside. It had a burnished gold light very similar to the clouds in his Sunday school books, and he saw it as a manifest sign of Jesus' love burning through nature.

With him he had a model tank, a truck, and a jet fighter to represent a rescue mission on a distant planet. Tommy went through the motions of the fantasy, evoking a trance in which he thought about his mother. He felt he had betrayed her by talking with Miriam, and soothed his loneliness by pretending her spirit was close by. The rescue went on apace in the exotic vegetation of the other world. All day his rear was hurting him, and now, as he knelt in front of the flowerbed, little stabs of pain pricked him where the belt had broken his skin. It reminded him of how careful he had been all day not to attract attention to himself at school. Whatever her motives, he was glad Miriam had punished him for the terrible thing he had done to the shepherd boy.

The earthy scent of the geraniums made him calm as he relaxed in the certain feeling that God was everywhere in the generous light. All one had to do to be absolved was to be open to forgiveness. He sat in reverie, unaware that Segundo had left the upper terrace or that he was being watched, until a couple of sheep bleated and he looked up.

They had moved away from the flock, standing idly by the side of the road where the dirt track met the pavement. The vision startled him, for as sympathetic as he was to animals, his reverie made him more impressionable than usual. His heart opened to the appearance of the bedraggled creatures under the warm light. A moment later he noticed the shepherd boy staring back at him as well. Somehow he no longer felt awkward toward his victim and decided to make up to the Indian boy. He felt courage surging into him from his mother, and realized the Kingdom of Heaven could be alive in that very garden, under the generous light. He said, "Hello," and held up his hand.

Chaco glared back at the gringo incredulously. Only yesterday the mother of the house had baited him with her gestures, gloating at him with laughter:

"Ha Ha Ha! Ha Ha Ha!"

The stern silence of the other boy brought a wave of guilt

to Tommy, and his awkwardness returned. He looked into the flowerbed, decided to make an offering to the boy, and held up the truck. There was still no reaction from the shepherd. Tommy noticed the boy had given up control of his flock for the opportunity to stare him down.

Chaco watched the offering with a wave of anger. It was clearly a boast: "*I* have a toy truck—and *you* don't!" A moment later the gringo picked something else up and held it higher.

"*I* have a tank!"

The arrogance of the blond was incredible. Chaco took in the fountains sparkling behind the boy, the images of the sky and clouds reflected on the windows of the house, and wondered at what the gringo was doing with all that great fortune behind him—making fun of someone with no hopes of his own, whom he had already wronged! Chaco was so overcome with humiliation that he squatted in the dirt as tears came to his eyes. But he gazed back at the little god and tried not to look hurt. The mongrel limped past the shepherd and sat on the sidewalk, licking his leg. At that moment the German shepherd charged up from the lower terrace and started barking through the rails of the fence. The mongrel was in too much pain to respond.

The little god lifted something else into the air.

"*I* have an airplane!"

This final boast was too much for the Indian, and he remembered, looking into the superiority of the gringo's face, the humiliation he had suffered because of him and the scar cast over the rest of his life. He stood up, feeling in his pockets for the slingshot and the rocks.

The first shot ricocheted off a grate in the fence and thudded into the imaginary world of the flowerbed. Tommy gazed at the stone with incomprehension and turned dumbly to the shepherd in time to see another rock loosed from the sling. The second shot hit him squarely above the right eye and split his eyebrow open. The impact left him even more bewildered. He didn't feel pain right away and continued staring as the Indian ran downhill ahead of the sheep and the flock began to scatter. Only the mongrel, who couldn't make up his mind about anything, remained in place.

After a couple of seconds the blood started running into Tommy's eye, and the real shock of the moment came to him. He got up and started running to the house with his hands over his brow, crying "Mommy! Mommy! Mommy!" But he stopped halfway to the door when he remembered what actually confronted him there. He remembered that his mother was dead. He stood there, cupping his eye with his hands.

O, she was dead. She was dead, and she would always be dead; and Jesus, on his throne in heaven, was very far away.

The End

About the Author

Darick Allan was born in Brazil and grew up in Latin America and Africa. He currently lives in Washington, D.C.